THE GALLOWS GHOST

Hanged for a crime he didn't commit, a man goes to his grave swearing revenge on all present. Then a 'ghost' in a black duster and skull face terrorizes the Texas Panhandle, exacting a hanged man's revenge. One by one, the members of the Forester Cattlemen's Association are murdered and a rancher's beautiful daughter is threatened. Can Luke Banner discover the shocking secret of the Texas Plains, or will he too become another victim of the Gallows Ghost?

Books by Lance Howard
in the Linford Western Library:

THE COMANCHE'S GHOST
THE WEST WITCH

LANCE HOWARD

◆

THE GALLOWS GHOST

Complete and Unabridged

LINFORD
Leicester

First published in Great Britain in 1997 by
Robert Hale Limited
London

First Linford Edition
published 1998
by arrangement with
Robert Hale Limited
London

British Library CIP Data

Howard, Lance
    The gallows ghost.—Large print ed.—
Linford western library
1. Western stories
2. Large type books
I. Title
823.9′14 [F]

ISBN 0–7089–5195–3

Published by
F. A. Thorpe (Publishing) Ltd.
Anstey, Leicestershire

Set by Words & Graphics Ltd.
Anstey, Leicestershire
Printed and bound in Great Britain by
T. J. International Ltd., Padstow, Cornwall

This book is printed on acid-free paper

Dedication:
In loving memory of
Bugsy Doodles Malone.
You never asked for anything
but affection and I could
never give you enough.
I'll miss you always.

1

THE Panhandle moon setting in a frosty ebony-and-ice-chip sky was a sorry sight to see for a man about to have a noose tightened around his neck.

Soon, false dawn would enamel the sky with grey, blotting out the stars. The moon would slip behind the horizon. And an innocent man's blood would stain guilty hands.

Bob Diller was no rustler, though to the eight men gathered by the creek, he was surely that. The sheriff and members of the Forester Cattlemen's Association had convicted him without benefit of a trial. It mattered little that Bob Diller had never stolen a longhorn in his life. All they saw was a tenuous trail of evidence someone had left pointing his way; in this parcel of the Texas Panhandle that was all the

1

proof they needed.

Bob struggled furiously against the men dragging him to the creek. He kicked out, nearly snapping the Circle H foreman's grip on his right arm. But the deputy clutching his left managed to hold tight while the foreman adjusted his hold. Gasping, muscles weak with exhaustion, his gaze lifted, locking on the huge cottonwood a few feet ahead. Its bulk shivered with marbled light from the flickering lanterns held by two of the other men present. Sallow light played over their faces, in their eyes, showing no warmth, no mercy, merely a consensus of grim determination, accusation. Hardened men, these, no-nonsense and stalwart; they would see this hanging through, "Get the job done," as Sheriff Ben Franklin had said when he ordered Bob Diller from his cell. Men of iron, eager to get home to their spreads and attend to the daily routine of running a cattle ranch — the threat of rustling presumably out of the way.

But it wouldn't be out of the way. Because they were hanging the wrong man.

"Bastards!" Bob shouted. "All of you!" The deputy grabbed a handful of Diller's hair and jerked his head up, forcing him to face the men present. One man stepped forward, holding up a lantern, shining buttery light over Bob's angular face. Lantern flame glittered from his eyes, reflected with fury and smothered panic. Yet no cowardice shown, no surrender. He refused to bow to these men, to their judgment. He would afford them his spite and denial, no more.

The man who came forward, Clayton Sharpe, had a jowly face showing sixty years of sun-baked leathery hide. He shifted his bulk from one foot to the other and surveyed the younger man and shook his head.

"You're a goddamn sorry piece of hide, Diller, you know that?" Sharpe's tone carried a false bravado, an attempt to mask a note of uncertainty that fell short. "You could at least do us all a favor and set our minds assured you done what you did."

Diller blew out a grunt of disgust and spat, catching the other man squarely in the cheek. Sharpe wiped it away with a sleeve, an angry gleam sparking in his eyes. "I ain't givin' you the satisfaction, Sharpe. I ain't guilty of nothin', not no rustlin', not even pissin' on your property. You're lookin' for an end to this cattle stealin', but it won't end 'cause you got the wrong fella and you know it. You best take a look at your own." For an instant, Diller's eyes cut to Sheriff Franklin.

Clayton Sharpe's lips turned with a smug expression, but doubt betrayed itself in his eyes. "You're our huckleberry, all right. God in Heaven, you gotta be."

"He's guilty as hell!" Dustin Harlow, the Circle H foreman, tightened his grip on Diller's arm and gave him a shake. "Evidence says so. Let's get this done."

4

"We'll know soon enough." Sheriff Franklin stepped up to the cottonwood and ran his gaze its length.

Franklin appeared every bit his namesake: a bald head, framed by long grey-streaked brown hair to either side, shone with reflected moonlight; wire-rimmed spectacles highlighted small, close-set eyes; his full face carried an avuncular look that belied the iron grip with which he held the small town of October Creek. Rumor had it he had hanged more than one man on less evidence than he'd collected on Diller.

Sheriff Franklin had a noose draped over his arm.

With a backward step he swung the noose in a tight circle, tossing it over a limb. He motioned to one of the ranchers, Bryce Merton — a wiry man in his late fifties — to lead the bay tethered to a bush beneath the noose.

As Merton guided the animal beneath the tree, a thin smile oiled Franklin's lips. He turned to Diller, stony gaze falling upon the younger man, who stared at the swaying noose, Adam's apple bobbing, eyes narrowing. He was going to die. He saw no way clear in appealing to these men for mercy, but he'd be damned if he'd give them total satisfaction. He believed powerfully in the law of circles and these men would pay for their actions.

"You got your peace to say?" Franklin fished paper and tobacco from his pocket and rolled a smoke. Puffing it to life, he held it out to Diller, who refused with a shake of his head. "Suit yourself." Franklin enjoyed this, was making a morbid show of it.

Diller's gaze swept from man to man: the deputy, Circle H foreman, Sharpe, Merton; the other ranchers, Jonathan Stiller, Cale Hadley, and Caleb Forester — leader of the Forester Cattlemen's Association. His gaze was cold, accusing, damning.

"I got only one thing to say to all of you. You're killin' an innocent man

6

and by all that's holy I swear you'll pay for it."

"Ain't too goddamn likely!" scoffed Harlow. "Devil's got a room all nice and picked out for the likes of you."

Diller sneered. "I'll be takin' the lot of you with me, by God, I swear it. I'll come back and hang you all."

The sheriff bellowed a laugh. "See, boys, he's done gone loco! That's crazy talk, Diller. I'd hang you on that alone, if'n you weren't guilty of rustlin'."

The sheriff nodded and the men dragged Diller to the horse. He kicked and fought, but he was exhausted and they were too strong for him. Franklin stepped up, drawing his Peacemaker. He swung it at the back of Diller's head and a loud *thunk* sounded. Diller slumped, shadow and moonlight streaking before his eyes. Holstering the gun, the sheriff looped a rope around Diller's hands, securing them behind his back. The deputy and foreman hoisted Diller into the saddle and slipped the noose around his neck.

The sheriff gazed up at him.

"What the devil you waitin' on, Sheriff?" asked Caleb Forester, a red-haired man with a rugged rancher's build. A look of concern and vague revulsion showed in his eyes.

The sheriff uttered a tinny laugh. "Want him to know it's happenin', Forester. Wanna see him dance."

"That's a little morbid, isn't it?" Forester shook his head, disgust turning his rugose features.

Franklin shrugged. "Reckon."

"Nooo!"

A scream ripped out and the sheriff spun, going for his gun; the others appeared frozen. A man, more a boy, rightly — he looked to be about sixteen — charged at them, swinging a rifle butt. The boy had the same gaunt features as Bob Diller, features made sharper by hate and cold fury. He swung the rifle butt in a looping uppercut at Franklin, who hadn't quite pulled his gun free and couldn't react fast enough to get out of the way.

The sheriff jerked his head sideways but the blow hit him at a glancing angle. Jumping a step backward, he cussed the night blue and spat a stream of blood.

By that time, the foreman and deputy broke their spell and charged the youth. The boy swung again and the deputy took the blow on the shoulder while the foreman arced a gloved fist at the boy's jaw. It hit, hard, sending him crashing to the ground. The rifle flew to the left; one of the ranchers snatched it up.

"Goddammit, Diller, you dang near brained me!" Franklin shouted, rubbing at the side of his face. A gash leaked a pencil-thin line of blood. Cold fury blazed in his eyes as his gaze locked on the boy. He walked up and kicked the youth square in the teeth. The boy blew out a spray of blood and fell back. Franklin cocked his leg for another kick, but Forester grabbed his arm.

"That's enough, Franklin. You can't blame the boy. It's his brother gettin' the necktie party."

9

Franklin's eyes narrowed. "Blame him, hell, I oughta kill the sonofabitch for that!" But Franklin backed off while the deputy and foreman hoisted the half-conscious youth to his feet.

Johnny Diller looked up with glazed eyes. "He ain't guilty, you bastard! You know it well as these others."

Franklin wiped a dribble of blood from his lip with the back of his hand. "He's guilty as a bargirl with the jiggers — hang 'im!" Franklin waved his hand, but not a rancher moved. Their gazes shifted from Franklin to the youth. "What the goddamn hell's wrong with y'all?" The sheriff drilled each rancher with a cold gaze, all of whom appeared uncomfortable and unsure.

"Ain't got the taste for executin', Sheriff," Sharpe ventured, shaking his head. "It's your job."

The sheriff uttered a choppy laugh. "Don't make you any less guilty, does it?" He moved towards the horse.

Johnny Diller screamed, tears running down his face.

Bob Diller looked at his brother, courage and resolve on his face. "Take care of yourself, Johnny. Get far away from here. Don't end up like this."

Franklin scoffed. "Yeah, boy, don't end up no cow thief or you'll be doin' the same dance."

Diller's gaze locked on Franklin, hate like hellfire in his eyes. "I'll make good on my promise, Sheriff. You'll pay for this. I'll come back to see you hang."

"Sure, you will, son." Franklin grinned. "And I'll have a whiskey waitin'." Franklin slapped the horse on the rump and let out a "Yah!" The bay bolted and Bob Diller jerked backward out of the saddle.

The noose drew taut.

The moon said a prayer.

And Bob Diller hanged.

* * *

A low-hanging mist shivered through the virgin grazeland of the *Llano Estacado*. It ghosted over the flat featureless expanse of buffalo grass and mesquite, slivers of moonlight skittering like opal genies within. Genies granting no wishes, only loneliness. It was brooding, eerie, night on the Plains. A night for ghosts.

Far in the distance the Canadian River snaked through the Staked Plains — once the domain of the mighty Comanche, all of whom had been forced on to reservations within the past two years by General Ranald Mackenzie and his Fourth Calvary. A forlorn place, domain of cattleman and rustler, Indian spirit and whispering wind, the Plains seemed to stretch on forever.

Every now and then the shadowy shape of a longhorn moved, its mournful cry lending to the ghostly aspect of the moon-glazed night. Many a cattleman claimed the Plains to be another world, a gateway to the spectral, the unknown — a sentiment Bryce Merton, staring out the huge double windows of the main house on his Bar M spread, could have echoed. The churning mist and opal moon drove home the things he felt — remorse, guilt, emptiness. He hated nights like this, especially since . . .

Merton shivered, trying to forget. Praying to forget. Funny, how many years had he felt comfortable living here? Too many to count. But all that ended six months ago. He couldn't recollect a day of comfort since they'd hanged that boy.

He recollected that night, that gnawing sense of wrongness, injustice, telling him they'd made an unrectifiable mistake. Normally he would never have given Franklin a lick of credibility, but they'd just been so all-fired intent on stopping the rustling, putting it to rest with the body that lay buried beneath the emerald grass near the creek. True, the rustling had stopped to all intents and purposes, but lately . . . lately he'd begun to suspect things weren't quite so cut and dried with cattle stealing as they'd believed.

Except for the Injun's, Merton's was the smallest of the Panhandle spreads, claiming merely a few thousand head.

He *would* notice it more, owning the smaller tract, wouldn't he? A few longhorns missing here, a few there. Larger spreads wouldn't notice as quick. Or maybe they'd simply ignore it, because to acknowledge the fact meant acknowledging they'd hanged an innocent man.

An innocent man.

Christamighty, he'd worried that bone endlessly over the past months. The boy did little to help matters. Diller's brother had made it his life's work jawing about the hanging. Every night in the saloon like clockwork, Johnny Diller told the tale to anyone who would listen. Merton wished to high hell the kid'd shut his mouth. It just made things worse, worse for Merton because of the spectre of guilt that haunted his dreams and worse for himself because nothing could bring Bob Diller back.

Bring Diller back.

Merton recollected Diller's dying words, words that tumbled like wraiths in the eerie atmosphere of the Plains: he'd come back. Take revenge.

Hell, a body could almost believe that load of cowflop on a night like this.

Merton tensed and listened intently a moment, hearing his own heart thud behind his ribs.

A sound?

Most of the Bar M's 'hands were in October Creek, getting their bells rung or losing their shirts. That left the damn spread virtually deserted, except for a few servants asleep upstairs. Deserted. That was a word Bryce Merton felt damned uncomfortable with at the moment.

He *had* heard something; he felt sure of that much. If not the 'hands, who? Or what?

The wind? That's what it had been, he assured himself, feeling little relieved. Nothing more, though as he glanced out into the darkness and saw the fog merely shiver he knew the night was damn near still. Yet what other explanation was there?

Bob Diller.

Godamighty! The name stung his thoughts. What if they had put an innocent man to death? Curse Franklin. He was so galldanged fired-up on pinning it on Diller.

Hell, there was evidence, wasn't there?

Merton didn't feel a lick less guilty.

Because it's still happening, you sorry old bastard! You can't deny those longhorns are missing.

No, he couldn't, but when he'd brought up the notion at the last cattlemen's meeting the others had brushed him off, saying, "Hell, you always got your sick'uns and wanderers. Perfectly natural to lose a few cows."

Natural, true, but Merton knew better.

There!

Merton started, beads of sweat

16

springing out on his forehead. No noise this time, but a *sight*. He had spotted movement beyond the stand of cottonwoods that shaded the ranch house. Quick, furtive movement, a flash of white.

A shiver rattled his spine and his hand drifted to the six-gun at his hip. Goddamn, he felt boogered for no particular reason he could figure. So he had seen something? Probably a hoot owl or some such.

A disturbing voice in his being warned him it was no owl and the sound that came next assured him of the fact.

A laugh. A shivery living thing, it rose and fell and chilled him to the bone. A ghost of guilt and remembrance haunted his mind.

Diller.

Holy God Almighty! Why had that name invaded his thoughts again? He wished he could force it away but it didn't matter, now. Something was out there, close to the house, and by God he had to deal with that threat.

Merton moved from the window and went to the door, easing it open. He peered out into the night, the opalescent fog. At first he saw nothing, but the laugh rang out again and a spike of panic pierced his mind.

"Oh Lord," he mumbled, drawing his gun, clenching it in a hand he fought to keep from shaking. He edged out on to the veranda and lifted the gun, shifting it left and right in a protective arc.

"Who's there?" he yelled. "Who's out there? Answer me or by God I'll fill you full of holes!"

Merton stepped on to the grass, all thoughts of hanging and guilt forced from his mind by the more immediate menace. He edged towards the cottonwoods.

A swish caught his attention and he spun.

His heart jumped into his throat. His hand set to trembling in earnest and panic seized his mind. Instantly thoughts of hanging and Bob Diller swarmed back.

He stared at the impossible, the unearthly. He was a practical man, forged by hard living and back-breaking toil, but all that was cast aside for Bryce Merton suddenly believed in ghosts as surely as he believed in the Lord God Almighty.

By the cottonwood, stood a figure, not exactly a man, but a *thing*, a thing from the darkest nightmare, a redman's peyote vision. Garbed in a black duster that hung open, moonlight glinting off a bowie knife and Colt at its hip, the figure mocked him. Black clothes, gloves and Stetson, hid its form. If it weren't for the face, Merton might well have missed the figure in the darkness.

The face. Could he call it that? No, not a face at all, not a man's at any rate. The face of a death's-head, a gleaming white skull, with hollow black eyes and grinning teeth, a ghastly visage. Merton swore he could see the outline of rope burns at the spectre's neck.

Dread coursed through him. For he saw death, his death. He mouthed a silent prayer, begging forgiveness.

The thing let out its shuddery laugh and Merton stiffened, taking a hesitant step. His gun hand shook. "Christamighty . . . " he mumbled. The apparition glided a few paces closer. "Diller, it's you, ain't it?"

"Told you I'd come back, Merton." The spook's voice came raspy, as though the hangman's rope had damaged his vocal chords. "Told all of you I'd come back."

The apparition took another step and Merton noticed something outlined in frosty moonlight behind it — a *noose*, slung over the branch of a cottonwood. A crate rested on the ground beneath it.

Merton shook his head, eyes widening. "No, Diller. It wasn't my fault, I swear it wasn't. Franklin arranged it, the whole thing. He said he had evidence."

The apparition laughed and the sound chilled Merton. "So? You were there. You were all there. You knew I wasn't guilty. You could have stopped it."

The thing leaped forward, swooping in like some great black bird of death. Merton fought to get the six-gun to aim, but panic froze him to the spot. Finger jerking, he managed to get off a shot just as the thing descended on him. The bullet went wide, drilling into the ground.

The ghost hit him and all feeling suddenly drained from his legs. He stumbled backwards, gun flying from his grip.

He went down, slamming his head against the edge of the veranda. His senses spun and speckles of light and darkness danced before his eyes. Powerless, he felt himself lifted, dragged to the cottonwood. In that moment he knew Bob Diller's terror on that night six months past. He muttered something about forgiveness and the ghost uttered a hoarse laugh.

"You should be more careful who you hang next time, Merton," the apparition said. "Sometimes the dead don't stay buried."

Merton felt himself lifted to his feet, legs shaky.

Something. Around his neck. Tightening.

The ground beneath him vanished. In a flash of terror he realized the figure had looped the noose about his neck and kicked the box from beneath his feet. Biting pain squeezed his neck. He struggled for breath, finding none. Through the thundering in his ears he heard a muffled peal of laughter, but it receded all too fast. In its place blackness rode in, a dark horse Bob Diller would have called vengeance.

★ ★ ★

Jonathan Stiller, owner of the Slash L, sat his horse by the creek and stepped from the saddle. Gazing out at the dark misty expanse of the Staked Plains, he wondered where the hell his cattle were getting off to. He had pegged the wanderers for the Circle H, figuring they had simply meandered over onto Forester's land, the way longhorns were wont to do, but now he wasn't so sure. Oh, only a handful were missing; he might not have even noticed if'n it weren't for Merton raising a stink at the last meeting, dredging up the old ghost of rustling.

Old ghost . . .

A thought struggled to form in Stiller's memory, quickly chased away. He didn't have time for such nonsense; he had steers to find.

Rustling.

A nagging notion, that. Galldammit, why couldn't he get rid of it? Merton, that's why. Damn him and his guilt. All right, he reckoned he felt guilty about Diller, too — hell, they all did. But guilt wouldn't bring him back and by dammit that boy *had* to be guilty.

They hadn't seen a lick of rustling for six months.

Maybe the thief had laid low?

Stiller's stern features set in hard lines. No, couldn't be. If cattle were vanishing it was a new menace. He wanted to blame it on wandering, but he had discounted that theory earlier today. Forester had agreed to let him check the Circle H spread for steers bearing the Slash L brand, but Stiller hadn't found a single cow that didn't belong to the man. He'd located no carcasses, neither, though that wasn't a particular surprise with the buzzards around these parts.

You made a mistake . . .

Shut the hellfire up, he scolded himself, guilt pricking him. What's done is —

Stiller jolted, a sound swarming up from the night. Behind him! A laugh, and a goddamn eerie one. He whirled, hand slapping for his Peacemaker.

It never made it. Something collided with his temple and his legs went out

24

from under him. He hit the ground hard, the night spinning with white and black streaks and sibilant laughter.

"You're gettin' your own necktie party, Stiller!" he heard someone say in a weird raspy voice. "Just the likes of which you gave me."

Through blurred vision, Stiller saw a figure doing something beneath a cottonwood. He wondered if he had hit his head harder than he thought because the figure appeared to have no body at first, merely a white head floating atop nothing. As his vision cleared, he realized the figure wore dark clothing and had no real face to speak of, merely a bleached skull with hollow black eyes and a death's-head grin.

"Judas Priest . . . " Stiller mumbled. The figure slung a rope over a branch, then led Stiller's own horse beneath. Stiller shoved aside all shock and concentrated on saving his hide. He was a controlled rigid sonofabitch who damn well didn't believe in such things

25

as ghosts and hanged men returning from the dead. Although he couldn't deny the being before him, he would deal with that after he escaped the menace threatening him now.

He struggled to push himself to his hands and knees, but before he got half-way, something collided with his jaw. Blood sprayed from his mouth. His mind reeled and he felt himself lifted, hurled forward. He stumbled against his horse, gripping the saddlehorn to keep himself upright. The ghostly figure grabbed him by the belt and heaved him into the saddle. Stiller had little strength to resist.

The figure slid the noose over Stiller's head.

"Goddammit, you'll burn in hell for this, Diller!" the ranch man managed to yell as his senses stopped spinning. His gaze settled on the apparition.

"Too late for that, Stiller, but don't you worry none, you'll have plenty of company by the time I finish."

The figure slapped the horse and Jonathan Stiller suddenly dangled in the air. A brittle *crack* sounded and the rancher's body spasmed, soon going still.

2

THE rising sun blazed in the Texas sky, gilding the Circle H compound with golden light. Diamond sparkles glinted off dew-beaded grass and glittered from windows. The spread boasted the largest number of beeves in the Panhandle and Caleb Forester owned it all — would own more with the news the sheriff had delivered this morning: Merton and Stiller were dead, hanged, and by arrangement and default of the Forester Cattlemen's Association the spoils — if a body could rightly call it that — would be divvied up among the remaining members, Merton and Stiller not being family men. Longhorn brands would be altered to fit the particular outfit by some expert Indian artist Forester hired, a trick gleaned from rustlers. The only thing Injuns were good for, in his mind. The thought tied to another matter, one involving his daughter, Shania, but he quickly forced it away.

The Circle H compound consisted of a handful of buildings arranged in an irregular oval beyond the main house. Corrals and sheds dotted its expanse, as well as outbuildings for blacksmithing, carpentry and storage. A sprawling bunkhouse, complete with combination kitchen and dining area, stood near the supply commissary.

Stands of cottonwoods shaded the main house, built in the fashion of a hacienda. A substantial dwelling of adobe, it sported bank-vault-thick walls and deep-set windows. Hewn rafters overhung a flat roof and the wide front door might better have suited a castle, which was just what Caleb Forester considered the place — his castle. A veranda skirted the length of the front, shadowed at the height of the day by the cottonwoods. A fitting tribute to a man who had started with a handful of steers and built himself an empire.

Caleb Forester had arisen before the roosters, the way he always did, though the sheriff's visit had shaved an hour off that. He reckoned the other ranchers had been ousted from their beds as well; Franklin would make a show of telling all. Bryce Merton and Jonathan Stiller had been found dangling from cottonwoods on their respective properties. The thought of it gave Caleb an uneasy feeling, made him think of . . . *hush*! he scolded himself. No need to bring that up.

Caleb Forester stepped from the house into the bright sunlight. He made his way to one of the corrals where longhorns would be held in preparation for the spring drive along the Western Trail to the railhead at Dodge, but thoughts of the drive were far from Caleb's mind at the moment.

He located Dustin Harlow, his foreman, at the corral, mending a fence rail. A coating of sweat glossed

Harlow's bare back, shining over rippling ropy muscle in the early morning sunlight. Harlow had made himself damn near indispensable in Caleb's opinion. Signing on to the Circle H a good seven months ago, he had exhibited a dogged adaptability and no little amount of know-how and talent. Though the man carried a hard edge Caleb wondered about at first, all fears were quickly distilled. Harlow's work proved exemplary, an inspiration to the 'hands.

"Mornin', Dusty." Caleb tipped his Stetson as he came up behind the foreman. Dusty Harlow twisted, gazing up at the older man, arching a hand above his eyes to shield them from the sun.

Harlow sported a build of average height packed with slabs of muscle. His arms looked powerful and his back was wide. Thick sinuous ropes of muscle sheathed his bull neck. A sharp nose and high cheekbones gave his face a stern look. Handsome in a rugged western way, he was no pretty-boy type like they had back East and Forester respected that. Harlow nodded, nails for the railing clenched between his teeth.

Caleb removed his hat and brushed red hair from his forehead. Forester himself was a large man, with a rugged rancher's build sixty years hadn't robbed him of and a no-nonsense look welded into his blue eyes. Composed of grit and a goodly measure of stubbornness, he was self-made in every sense of the word.

"Wanna talk with you a moment, son." Forester motioned for Harlow to follow him to the end of the corral. Harlow shrugged and spat the nails into his hand, laying them aside. He trailed after the older man.

"Saw some of the boys headin' out with rifles damn early, Caleb." Harlow leaned on a post and brushed his hands on his jeans.

Caleb nodded, face serious. "That's what I aim to talk to you about. Seems we had us a bit of trouble late last night."

"Don't say?" Harlow cocked an eyebrow. "What kind of trouble — rustlin'?"

Caleb shook his head, look going from serious to grim. "Killin's. Bryce Merton and Jon Stiller got their necks stretched."

Harlow's face took on a look of surprise. "Whatchu mean? I didn't hear 'bout no charges on them."

"T'weren't that. Someone took it upon himself to hang those men in cold blood. Far as I know, neither had done nothin' shady, so murder's all it could be."

"Robbery?" Harlow scratched his head.

Caleb shrugged. "Nope, nothin' taken, not a single damn steer, nor nothin' inside. Sheriff came and told me about it this mornin' afore the crack of dawn. Imagine he told the rest and now we got some cattle to divvy up."

"Always use more."

"Not that way. Prefer to get my beef by barter, buy or birth, as the sayin' goes."

"This way's the same, just a bit peculiar."

"Reckon you're right, but I'd rather have them alive. It worries the hell out of me, son."

"Why should it?" Harlow looked perplexed. "Don't see as how those men being killed relates to the Circle H."

"Maybe it don't, but I got a feelin' somethin' like that's bound to spill over. Those men were killed for some particular reason and if it weren't robbery then it was something more worrisome. I wouldn't be surprised none if all us ranchers might be in for a heap of trouble and I aim to divert it."

Harlow straightened, gazing out at the spread. "How you aim to do that, Caleb? I mean, Sheriff have any idea who done it?"

"Looks like one of the ranch 'hands might have spotted the hombre, ridin' away. One of Merton's men was returnin' early from a poker game in October Creek, when he saw someone ridin' hell-bent into the night."

"That ain't much help."

"No, but he told the sheriff a mighty strange tale."

"Strange, how? A killer's a killer. Ain't seen much difference in the breed."

"This killer was different, the man said. He was all decked out in black."

"So?" Harlow made a doubtful face.

Forester's eyes shifted. He felt damned uncomfortable talking about it in the light of day. "Looks like the killer had no real face to speak of, the man said."

Harlow let out a laugh. "Too much rotgut! You know that saloon. Surprised the fella found his way home!"

Forester shook his head, frowning. "No, Sheriff said the man hadn't drunk more than a whiskey or two. That's what scares the beejesus outa me."

"How so?" Harlow still looked puzzled.

"Man tells the tale as how the killer had no face, just a skull under a black Stetson, like he was some kind of spook or somethin'."

"Pshaw! Ain't no goddamn such."

The lines in Caleb's forehead deepened. "That's what I used to think, now I wonder. Man said this thing had a laugh that would scare the meat off a set of bones."

"Caleb, I ain't never known you to be one to subscribe to such foolishness. Always had you pegged as a man with his feet firmly on the soil."

Caleb Forester stiffened, suddenly annoyed and embarrassed. Spooks. Harlow was right: God honest crazy talk, that's what it was. Yet he couldn't help thinking it.

Caleb drew a deep breath. "Got my feet there. But I took to wonderin' 'bout what Merton was sayin'."

Harlow's face grew serious. "'Bout rustlin'?"

"Yep, 'bout that. What if we hung that Diller fella by mistake?"

Harlow grunted. "You think old Diller's spook done come back to take revenge, way he promised?"

Caleb's ruddy face turned a shade redder. He didn't cotton to the sarcasm in Harlow's tone, but he reckoned it was to be expected. Caleb would have done the same thing had he stopped to think about what he was saying. "Maybe I don't know what I'm talkin' about." He shook his head. "But I do know trouble and right now I can sniff it out of the air like a blue norther. It's comin', Dusty, and it's comin' hard."

"Said you aim to do somethin' about it — that why you sent the men out?"

Caleb's head lifted and he looked out across the spread. "Told them to place themselves at strategic points, look out for anything . . . unusual."

"Like spooks with skull faces?" Harlow's ill-placed humor was lost on Caleb.

"Maybe. Or maybe just another killer

tricklin' out of Indian Territory, lookin' for some steers to sell the Injuns. Whatever it is, I want to be ready for it."

"You got 'em out at night?"

Caleb nodded. "I'll have them there 'round the clock if that's what it takes. But that ain't the whole of it."

"Meanin'?" Harlow's eyes narrowed to a squint.

"Hired me someone."

It was Harlow's turn to tense. "Who?"

"A manhunter; someone who ain't bound by the local law. Sheriff can't be trusted, we all know that, and he won't make no effort to find the killer. So I'm takin' matters into my own hands."

"That's going a little far, ain't it, Caleb? I hear them manhunters got no soul or conscience a body can tell. More trouble than they're worth, if you ask me."

"Maybe so, but I don't rightly see a choice. I'm a hard man, Dusty, but I admit my mistakes and I don't let my friends down. Stiller and Merton deserve to rest in peace. That means findin' their killer."

"What if it's Diller's spook come back for revenge?" A glint of cold humor sparked in Harlow's hard eyes.

"Well, then that's a mistake I'll have to reckon with. Spook or no, the man I hired will put an end to it."

Harlow licked his lips. "This man got a name?"

"Luke Banner."

Harlow's eyes widened and he jerked straight as a rail post. "Holy Christ, Caleb! You know the reputation that hombre's got?"

Caleb nodded. "Best in the business, I hear tell."

"Yeah? I heard he done turned on a couple of men who hired him on, shot them clean twixt the eyes for no reason other than to see them die."

"Load of cowflop. Those men were guilty of crimes and tried to pin it on someone else. They drew on him."

Harlow cocked an eyebrow. "How

you know that, Caleb? I heard men got a funny way of drawin' on him, least that's what he claims."

Forester waved off Harlow's words. "Had him checked out a while back when I was thinkin' of hirin' him on to take care of the rustlin'. Law let him free after those incidents, so that's good enough for me."

"What if he turns on us?"

"Why should he? We ain't guilty of nothin', 'cept maybe a mistake hanging Diller. Was the sheriff who convicted him, so he can't hold us accountable."

"Some goddamn mistake. He might not see things the same way." Harlow got a look of worry on his rugged face. Forester could well see the man's point, but this thing had him boogered and he damn well had to take the chance. He'd never been one to sit on his saddle.

"No choice, way I see it, Dusty. I got more than just a cattle business to protect. I got Shania to look out for. I won't take the risk of some killer gettin' in here and threatenin' her life."

Harlow nodded, face softening. "Agree with you there, Caleb. Be right beside myself anything happened to her."

Caleb gave Dusty a pat on the shoulder. "So when you gonna get hitched to her, son?" He laughed. "Time's a wastin'!"

Harlow grinned. "Soon as she says yes, Caleb. We still got that little problem with Silverbird."

Caleb's face reddened. "Ain't gonna be no problem. No daughter of mine's gonna marry no goddamned 'breed, no two ways 'bout it. She better get that damn fool notion outa her ornery skull. That boy will be crushed soon as I see fit if'n she keeps that tact."

Harlow chuckled. "Funny, she's says you're the ornery one, Caleb."

Caleb laughed as well. "I am a stubborn old cuss, true enough, but I'm set on that point."

"Why not get rid of Silverbird, now? He ain't got much land and only a few hundred head. Ain't part of the Association, neither."

Caleb shook his head. "Reckon I got a misplaced system of honor on that concern, Dusty. I recollect I only had few hundred head when I started out and I hate to squash the boy, 'breed or not — but make no mistake, Shania keeps her designs on gettin' hitched to him and I won't hesitate to drive him from the Panhandle. I don't aim to have no half-breed grandchild!"

"Agree with you there, Caleb. 'Course I got a vested interest."

Caleb slapped Harlow on the back. "You got a future wife, son, don't you forget that. I'll see to it you get a piece of this spread, too; call it a wedding present, but you gotta come through for me and marry Shania."

"Do my best, Caleb, surely I will — if'n I have to talk to that no-good 'breed myself."

A shot thundered through the early morning stillness. Caleb Forester and Dustin Harlow jolted, heads swiveling in the direction of the sound — the creek!

"Christamighty!" Harlow ran a hand over his chin.

"Looks like we got ourselves an unwelcome visitor." Caleb adjusted on his hat. "Maybe we got lucky and won't need that manhunter . . ."

3

LUKE BANNER eyed the rising sun and shook his head; he'd seen far too many dawns in his estimation and he was getting damned tired of it. At times he watched the sun edging over the horizon with a mixture of dismay and even disgust, wondering why he'd bothered to wake up to another day, another day that would likely be the same as countless others in a never-ending stream fostered upon him by the life he had chosen.

The life of a manhunter.

Manhunter, bounty hunter, gun for hire — call it what you would, but rightly it could be called legal murder. A licence to kill. That's what it boiled down to, killing, pure and simple. He'd never deluded himself otherwise. He saw it in men's eyes every time they faced him, innocent or guilty: *killer*.

Some men showed fear, some revulsion; none showed respect or understanding, but he had never expected as much.

Killer.

The word tortured him in weak moments, caused him to question his soul. Was he a man? Or was he an inhuman thing that did its job without remorse or guilt? A little of both? He reckoned so.

Would *she* have wanted him to put a bullet through every hardcase unlucky enough to cross his trail? every killer he blamed for taking life from him? No, she was much too kind for that. Too gentle. He was neither, not any more.

Those men were right. He was what he was. A killer. And that's just what a man named Caleb Forester had hired him to do.

Forester could consider himself lucky. Banner had just tied up a job involving horse thieves that had taken him into the bowels of Indian Territory, just north of the Panhandle. When he made a supply stop at his temporary base at a small town in the Panhandle, a telegram, forwarded by his secretary at the agency, had been waiting for him. Urgent, the missive said, pleading for a speedy answer. Something about two ranchers being murdered by a mysterious something-or-other. Banner might well have been inclined to ignore the telegram if it weren't for two simple facts: Caleb Forester was a man with a reputation, known far and wide as a power in the Panhandle cattle trade and because of the note of mystery attached to the job. Though bone weary from his previous job, the missive had piqued his interest.

He wondered about Forester. It must be something damn perplexing to make the head of the Forester Cattlemen's Association bow to another's skills and direction. Range detectives came a penny a dozen and usually worked for the brand. To hire an outsider meant Forester was plumb buffaloed and knew it. And there was the rest of the Association to consider. They might not agree with the extreme measure of hiring a professional killer; Forester would surely not have had time to arrange a meeting for something that had occurred only a few hours ago, as the telegram had indicated. Forester was willing to take any heat for the decision on his own.

Forester would not expect him so soon. The rancher had no way of knowing Banner was in the area and would figure on a few days for a response. Good. He preferred it that way. It gave him a chance to scout the premises, get a feel for the surroundings. Banner had a bit of the Indian in him, the cautiousness of finely honed instinct, refined by years on the trail chasing down men who defied the law, mocked justice. It meant staying alert, knowing the lay of the land. The smallest slip meant instant death and he'd come closer to that more times than he cared to count.

He shifted in the saddle. Was he looking for death, courting it, waiting for it to put an end to the loneliness he seldom let himself feel?

Why don't you settle down, you old buzzard?

Settle down. Make himself a normal life. A laugh, that, surely it was, merely the Devil's idea of a joke. He had lost that chance once. His only chance.

Banner drew up, lifting his Stetson and wiping a thin line of sweat from his brow. He scratched at the grey-flecked stubble on his chin. His face was lined, craggy, handsome yet worn by countless memories and the ghosts of the men he had killed. His frame was sturdy and powerful despite the age now creeping in — he'd be forty soon but felt a good ten years older. Numerous scars criss-crossed his hide, one high on his cheekbone.

His cold grey eyes set on the landscape, an endless emerald ocean of virgin grass sparkling with dew in the newborn sunlight. In the distance he spotted a creek, cottonwoods skirting its bank. That would give him a chance to stretch before making the final leg of his journey to the Circle H.

The Circle H. He contemplated it, wondering about men such as Forester. The rancher had it all — wealth, respect, power. Rumor had it he had the prettiest daughter east of the Pecos. Yet something was missing, something tenuous and unreachable that drove such men to acquire more and more. Banner realized he was making a judgement on a man he didn't know, but he had run into too many of the like not to get a handle on them. They were basically all the same. They started out so driven by the lust for power and money that even after they reached their goals they couldn't stop. A fever gripped them, an insidious subtle thing. Perhaps it was the power, the desire to reign over men less fortunate by luck or fate, or perhaps it was some demon buried in their soul.

Banner well knew the type; the same devil chased him. By all standards he was a wealthy man, could have bought a suitable spread and settled into a life of cattle ranching had that been his desire. He employed a secretary and occasional operatives, kept a hefty nest egg tucked in banks scattered across the country. He no longer needed this life. Yet some ghost drove him on.

He possessed near everything Forester did — money, power over other men, yet it wasn't enough. He was damned if he could tell anyone why.

Luke Banner uttered a low laugh and heeled his bay into an easy gait. He rode until he reached the creek and reined to a halt. Stepping from the saddle, he stretched and hung his hat on his saddlehorn. He went to the creek and knelt, splashing water into his face.

Sighing, he peered at the rippling water, which stilled, showing him the haggard reflection of a man too long on the trail.

You're a damned ugly sonofabitch, he told himself, though God knew enough women — women of questionable reputations and morals, but women nonetheless — assured him different. He wondered if he were peering at the reflection of his face, or of his soul.

He stood and started to turn — just as a bullet ploughed into the ground beside his feet. It kicked up a chuck of dirt and he froze, mind flashing with thoughts. Where had his damned sixth sense, the one honed to a razor edge by nights under the stars and days under the baking sun, gone? Why had it deserted him? Exhaustion? Maybe; though little made up for the fact that someone had just taken a shot at him and he was now in a hell of a bind.

Banner's gaze dropped to the holster secured by a thong to his thigh. His Peacemaker rested on an empty chamber. His rifle was tucked in its saddleboot, ten feet away. He'd get to neither in time to do him any good.

That left him in an unenviable position — waiting for the sniper's next move. He edged around, keeping his hands in plain sight.

A second shot did not come on the heels of the first; that was a good sign. He had enemies, God only knew how many, but he felt reasonably sure no one had followed him. No one but his secretary and the telegram operator knew where he was headed, and when. And it was damned unlikely an enemy would have missed the first shot.

No, the shot had been fired as a warning. It told him to go slow, make no sudden moves. An amateur, judging by the fact the man was waiting for him to make the first move. It made sense. Forester didn't know he was on the way and would likely have guards posted. Fingers would be itchy in light of the circumstances, the compound tense.

Movement caught his eye. To the side.

"Come on out," he said.

A hesitation, then a man stepped from behind a huge cottonwood, levering a Winchester at Banner's chest.

"Mornin'." Luke kept all emotion

off his face. His tone came steady and friendly. He surveyed the man: the fellow wore work clothes and gloves; a leathery quality to his face and thick build indicated someone used to doing manual labor. A cowhand, Banner pegged him for.

"Who're you?" The man lifted the rifle slightly.

"Name's Luke Banner, son."

"Banner? Ain't you that manhunter I heared so much about?" The man's eyes glossed with a sort of perverted reverence and Banner felt disgust well. He hated running into folk who took him to be more than he was, hated the legend fashioned around him by no-account pulp writers. Some fellas, like Cody, thrived on the attention; he did not. He reckoned it would get him killed one day.

"Sorry to say, I am. Ain't nothin' to be proud of."

The cowhand shook his head. "Hell it ain't! I heared you brought down near a hunnert men, read it in one of them dime books. You're somethin' of a hero of mine."

Banner frowned. "Ain't no hero to no one, son. What I done ain't no more than a job, a goddamn ugly one that no one else wants to do. Killin' a man . . . well, maybe it should be God's work. Reckon I fall far short of that."

The man gave him a puzzled look and lowered the rifle. "What you doin' here? You lookin' for someone?"

Awe shone in the man's eyes and Banner felt the sudden desire to knock it out of him; he'd become far too touchy about that sort of thing.

"Came here to do a job. On my way to the Circle H."

"Tarnation! I work for the Circle H! Was posted to make sure that killer didn't show up. You after him?"

"Depends on how your boss sees things. If I like what he tells me and he can meet my price, well, I'm here for the killer, then."

"Hot damn!" The man practically

54

did a dance. "I'll take y'all to him."

"Be much obliged." Banner went to his bay and put on his hat. Stepping into the saddle, he shook his head and wondered just what the hell he was getting himself into and longing for a day when nobody knew who the tarnation he was.

* * *

The parlor of the main house looked fancy yet simple at the same time. The walls were adorned with damn little, just one painting by some French artist Banner had never heard of. The furniture — settee and plush comfortable chairs, a couple of dark wood tables with fancy ball feet — appeared solid and expensive, little worn. The abode was freshly painted and a rich oval carpet lay on the polished floor. No clutter just clean and spacious, practical, if a bit impressed with its very sparseness.

It told Banner something about

the man before him. Caleb Forester mirrored his surroundings, sparse of emotion and feeling, practical, but used to wealth, comfortable with it. Banner knew his earlier estimation of the type had hit dead on: Forester, though he had plenty, was the type to be never truly satisfied; he would keep acquiring, keep asserting his dominance over men and situations. He would bow to Banner for one thing only — something he felt he had no control over. All else would be by the book.

That made no never mind to Banner. He couldn't change the type had he wanted to, and he wouldn't because that meant he'd have to start with himself.

He studied the other men in the room, the 'hand who had brought him here and Dustin Harlow, the Circle H foreman. The 'hand impressed him as starry-eyed, maybe a trifle slow. Forester dismissed him with a wave of his hand. The foreman on the other hand . . . Banner didn't like him particularly. He couldn't say why, only that he'd developed an aversion to him instantly and felt sure the foreman returned the sentiment.

Forester's gaze settled on the manhunter. "Didn't expect you so early, Banner. Lucky for you my man didn't shoot you. You should have told me you were coming today." Forester said it in a businesslike manner that held little reproach. He was used to ordering men around.

Banner went to the window, peered out, turned back to Forester. "Like to come in unannounced."

"Wonder you ain't been killed." Harlow moved to the settee and sat on an arm, hat in hand.

"Imagine so." Banner kept a measure of ice in his tone. "But I manage to keep alive, leastways have up to this point."

Forester grunted and waved off the conversation with a brusque motion of his hand. "Let's get on with it."

Banner nodded. "I'm all for that.

Why did you call me here, Forester?"

"Two ranchers were killed last night — "

"By a spook." Harlow put in, a smug expression on his face and sarcasm in his voice.

Banner's eyebrow cocked. "Do say?"

Caleb Forester explained the killings, going into no little detail about the supposed apparition with a skull face that had hanged the ranchers. When he finished, he peered at the manhunter and Banner had the sense the man was waiting for some sort of judgement, approval or just plain ridicule.

Banner gave him neither. "Whelp, you got my attention, Forester, I'll give you that much. Can't say I've run into anything similar."

"Pshaw!" said Harlow. "Plain foolishness!"

Banner eyed him, then the rancher, who gave the foreman a shushing look. The foreman didn't believe the story about a skull-faced hangman, it was plain to see, but Forester seemed to.

"You'll take the case?" Forester asked, expectant.

Banner tilted his head. "I'm interested."

"It's settled, then. You'll start immediately. I've got a room all set for you upstairs."

Banner nodded. "A hundred a day and fifty steers delivered to a man named Jay Lightheel in Indian Territory."

Forester's face turned red. "Jesus! You can't be serious?"

The foreman's face dropped, mouth opening.

Banner shrugged. "Dead serious. Take it or leave it. Reckon you got more steers than you can rightly use and an Indian friend of mine did me a turn on my last case. His family can use the help and I always remember my friends. The rest is my standard fee."

Forester shook his head. "That's goddamn robbery!"

"I agree, Mr Forester," said the foreman, standing. "We don't need this man."

Banner set his hat atop his head and

took a step towards the door. The case interested him but he'd set his terms and knew Forester could afford to meet them. Forester appeared more flustered than Banner would have figured him to be.

"Wait!" snapped Forester. The manhunter turned, eyeing him. The rancher regained some of his usual controlled confidence. "I'll agree to your terms, Mr Banner. But by God, you better find this . . . man."

Banner nodded. "I'll find him, and rest assured he is a man. Nothing more. Ain't come across the likes of a spook on the trail yet."

"Maybe you wouldn't be so sure if . . . " Forester appeared on the verge of saying more, but stopped himself.

Banner studied the man, drawing a conclusion. "You've got more to your story, Forester. What is it?"

The rancher shook his head and a look passed between him and his foreman. Whatever that something was it would remain unsaid.

"Just find this man, Banner, and at a hundred a day don't take your sweet time doin' it."

A strained silence fell over the room, suddenly broken by a footfall on the stairway leading to the upper floor. Banner glanced up to see a woman standing on the top step. A blue dress hugged her shapely figure, accentuating her ample breasts and natural curves. As she descended he noticed her striking blue eyes, the speckling of freckles dotting skin as smooth and clear as peaches. Soft tresses of red hair fell over her shoulders. A vision; she was probably the second most beautiful woman he'd ever seen. Weren't many a time he caught himself at a loss for words, but had anyone asked him his name just then he'd have been hard pressed to think of it.

The woman came into the parlor, glancing at the rancher and Banner, but avoiding Harlow.

"My daughter, Mr Banner, Shania." Forester said it with an ample amount of pride and rightly so.

"Ma'am." He tipped his hat.

"Shania and Dusty here aim to be hitched soon."

The woman forced a smile but Banner noticed a sudden dagger of anger in her eyes. By the same token a look of eagerness crossed the foreman's. He took the notion a mighty big difference of opinion on the idea of marriage existed between the two, but that wasn't his worry. He had a job to do.

"I'd like to get started, Forester. I'd appreciate directions to the ranches of the hanged men."

Shania gave her father a look of surprise.

"Mr Banner's just hired on to track Stiller and Merton's killer," he informed his daughter.

"A detective?" asked Shania. Then a smug expression turned her lips. "Or a killer himself?"

Her father cast her a reproachful look; she giggled.

"Possibly both," put in Harlow in acidic tone.

Forester ignored the remark and turned to Banner. "Tell Hinkley, the 'hand who brought you in, that I want him to take you over to the Stiller and Merton spreads. He's at your disposal."

"Thank you kindly." Banner tipped his hat to Shania and went for the door. He had the feeling he'd find damn little at the spreads but needed a place to start and that would be it.

4

LUKE BANNER sat in the darkness of the parlor, contemplating the day. Hinkley had given him a guided tour of the Stiller and Merton spreads, yet a careful search of the houses and grounds yielded nothing. He discovered tracks aplenty, far too many to distinguish a trail left by a lone killer.

He pondered the 'ghost' aspect of the case. He had to admit it was a new one on him. While it seemed silly in light of the mundane workaday world of the cattle rancher, he took it seriously. Ghosts. An impossibility in his book. A spectre garbed in black with a skull face. A spectre who hanged innocent men. Though he refused a supernatural explanation, he couldn't deny something unusual had occurred. For the moment, however, he needed to focus on the facts of the case.

Why had those men been hanged?

The question hung in his mind and he recollected the look that had passed between Forester and Harlow. They were hiding something, but what? Was it important to the case? Banner would find out soon enough. He always did.

What next? At this point he had little to hang a hat on. A ghost, two dead ranchers and no leads. Most cases he signed on to came with obvious motives — robbery, feuds, jealousy. This one appeared to have none of those. Still it had to be there.

His thoughts settled next on Harlow. The foreman was a horse of a different color. Banner didn't like him, but he couldn't convict him on personal taste. Plenty of men rubbed him the wrong way and he needed to look at things professionally. The foreman appeared hardened, but so were many such men throughout the West. Ranch workers were men forged by scorching suns and endless toil. They worked hard and lived harder; Harlow was cast pretty much along those lines. His intentions towards Forester's daughter were plain, though Shania Forester obviously didn't reciprocate. Did she feel the same aversion Banner did? Or were there other factors involved?

Banner's gaze drifted to the window. He peered out into the shadowy moonlit night. Ghosts and goblins, cattle and cattlemen. An odd combination.

Questions with no answers and his thoughts felt tangled. Exhaustion had caught up with him, yet he'd found himself unable to sleep. How many times had that occurred at the end of a case? How many times had her memory forced its way into his mind? He felt it there, waiting for him to sleep, to dream, and he reckoned if he were afraid of anything on this earth that was it. That was one ghost he was forced to believe in. Her ghost.

A sound broke his reverie. He looked towards the stairs, seeing a figure, barely visible in the gloom, coming down. Forester's daughter.

The woman made every effort to be silent. She glided down the stairs and across the foyer like a wraith. Shania Forester was plainly up to something but whatever it was seemed little concern of Luke Banner's.

She didn't spot him as she passed and he didn't stir. Opening the door, she stepped out into the night. Banner wondered where she was off to at this late hour and half-considered following her. He decided against it. She was a grown woman and he had been hired to find a killer, not baby-sit. Forester had guards posted, so he reckoned she'd be safe enough. She appeared adept at sneaking out of the house so he concluded it wasn't the first time.

He lifted out of his chair and went to the window. Peering out, he caught sight of the girl as she scooted off behind the cottonwoods and headed across the fields.

He was about to go back to his chair when something caught his attention.

His gaze shifted to the bunkhouse, spotting a hint of movement there. A figure slipped out, stocky build outlined in the pale moonlight. Harlow.

Banner sighed, any ideas of a comfortable bed and uninvolvement going to the wind. This changed the equation. Harlow was following Shania instead of meeting her and likely that meant trouble. Not the kind Banner had been hired for, but a chance to postpone his dreams.

He moved away from the window, grabbing his hat from the table beside the chair. He didn't know what Forester's daughter and the foreman were up to, but he aimed to find out.

★ ★ ★

Shania Forester hurried across the grass. A twinge of nervousness stabbed her belly at being out this late. Normally she gave the notion no thought but with the murders . . .

It didn't matter. She had to risk it.

68

Sneaking out at night was the only way she could see Jim, be with the man she intended to marry. Her father would be asleep and if he ever discovered her absence he'd take measures to see to it they were never together again. She couldn't allow that. Whether her father approved, she would marry Jim Silverbird and there was nothing he could do about it.

She sighed in exasperation. What made her father so all-fired set against the marriage? She'd asked herself that a hundred times, never finding a suitable answer. Jim owned a small tract of land, good solid land; the spread would grow, prosper, she felt sure, and someday the name of Jim Silverbird would be known throughout the Panhandle, right beside her father's. If only her father would give his blessing it would happen that much sooner.

He'd never give that blessing, would he? Caleb Forester hated Indians with a hate Shania could never begin to understand. It mattered little Jim was only *half* Cherokee. Her father branded all Indians the same. Savages, heathens, any number of dreadful things he chose to call them. She wondered what had turned him so bitter. He'd never talked of it, calling her notions of equality for all so much progressive fool-headedness. Didn't he know the West was changing? The Indian Wars were virtually over; most of the tribes had been herded on to reservations — out of sight, she called it, stuck away where whitemen wouldn't have to acknowledge their guilt — where they lived in squalor. A sorry existence for such a proud people. She knew Indians and she knew men: there was good and bad in any race; she understood that, though to her father's thinking there was good and there was Indian. She had never asked her father about his hatred, but it didn't matter; his hate wasn't hers. Her mind was made up. She loved Jim Silverbird and that was that.

Shania uttered a nervous laugh,

peered about. For an instant she got the uneasy feeling someone was following her. Just a feeling, a prickle down her spine, nothing as substantial as a footfall, or any sound for that matter. She halted, turned, scanning the landscape. No one. It was possible to lie flat in the grass and be concealed, especially at night, but she assured herself she was just being silly. She shivered, chastising herself for it.

All that talk of spook killers! It had her frightened over nothing. She was a grown woman, all of twenty-one, and she'd had her feet firmly on the ground since she was twelve, since her mama died and she'd become the woman of the house, though if Caleb Forester had his way she'd stay a little girl forever. She knew better than to believe in such pish-posh.

Didn't she?

Of course she did. Shania gave an uneasy chuckle and started forward again, heading for the creek a few hundred yards in the distance. Jim would be there, waiting. She prayed no one had seen her leave the house, reckoned no one had or she'd know it by now. Still, with that new man around and the guards posted . . .

She knew the cowhands' habits, knew when to risk sneaking out. But the new guy, Banner, she knew little about him. Fact was her first impression had been one of ambiguity. He had shown her little of what lay behind his cold eyes. A deadness lived there, a lack of compassion and humanity. Did he care about anything? Anyone? Or did he merely kill without remorse? She could read cowhands and tinhorns alike with the deft ease a cattleman read longhorns. The men she met were mostly alike, their desires and souls transparent to her. Banner was different. If he had a soul it lay hidden. He had been attracted to her, that much she could tell. Few men weren't. But that was all she could read. Banner was a man all too used to hiding feeling and thought. She supposed a man who killed others for a living would have to be. Manhunting was uncivilized in her opinion, though she realized necessary in this neck of the woods. Otherwise rustlers and the like would be escaping the law into Indian Territory all the time. Peaceful ranchers wouldn't be safe. She wished there was another way, but what could she say? She was merely a woman and in the West that made her opinion worth very little to hard-headed men like her father.

Well, damn him! she thought with a flash of bitterness, because there was one thing he wouldn't control: he wouldn't tell her whom she could marry. If he had his way she'd be gettin' hitched to that foreman, Harlow, a man she despised just by virtue of her father's insistence on their union. Imagine being married to the likes of that . . . that, well, she didn't know what but there was something about the man she just didn't care for. She s'posed he was handsome enough in a hard sort of way. And her father was prepared to turn over a substantial parcel of land and a goodly number of cows to start them off. Dustin Harlow had all the attributes of a stand-out cattleman and with Caleb Forester's help he'd be able to provide a good life for them. Many a frontier woman would have jumped at the chance, but she loved Jim and Harlow's potential aside, she plain didn't like the man.

Shania sighed, slowing as she neared the creek. Shadowy cottonwoods looked like skeletons, branches reaching out charred bony fingers. A shiver worked down her spine when she looked at them and thought about the skull-faced killer who'd hanged Stiller and Merton. The gurgling voice of the creek and chattering of katydids helped ease her apprehension and the thought of Jim gave her resolve. Hopeful, she scanned the area. She saw nothing at first, but expected as much. His Indian blood served him good stead and he would hide until he felt sure no one had trailed her.

She made her way down the sloping bank and whispered, "Jim?" eagerness in her heart.

Shania started as a hand touched her shoulder. She spun, a gasp escaping her lips.

"You damn near scared three years off my life!" she scolded, fighting to get her heart out of her throat.

"Wouldn't want to do that, least not 'fore I married you!" said the young man standing before her. Moonlight outlined his sharp handsome features — high cheekbones and sculptured face, dark hair and eyes, the smooth coffee-colored skin of a Cherokee. Shania wondered if that made it worse for her father, that Jim looked fully Indian though he was half Irish. She didn't care, and figuring out her father's narrow-mindedness was a job for a woman stronger than herself.

She gazed into his eyes, kissed him deeply, letting herself be lost in his touch, in his arms. "I wish it could be now, Jim," she whispered. "I wish we could just run off and be married and that would be the end of it."

The young man sighed, drawing her closer. "You know it can't be that way. I want your father's respect, not his hate. I'll find a way to earn that somehow. I thought the cattle ranch would do it, but he wants something more."

"He wants something you can't give." She buried her head in his shoulder. "I know my father. I know he's carried this hatred for Indians since I can remember. I don't even know why, but it's too strong to break."

"Maybe it is, but he could have crushed me by now if he'd taken a notion to do so. But he hasn't, so I have to believe there's a chance things will work out."

"How long, Jim?" Shania's voice turned pleading. "How long will you wait? I can't stand much more. He's pressuring me to marry Harlow. It's going to come to a head soon."

"It won't be long, I promise. I'll

give it a spell, but not indefinitely. If it doesn't work, we'll try it your way, but not before the fall. At least give me that long."

She gazed into his eyes with a look of resignation. She longed to be done with all this, run away with him and live a life in Wyoming or some such place where they could start anew, where they could live poor, but together. But she knew he was right: he had built what he had built *here*. Running from her father wasn't the answer — unless all else failed.

"All right. I promised to wait and I will. But I can't help longing, Jim. I can't help it a lick."

"I know — "

A heavy thud snapped his words short. Jim Silverbird suddenly went limp in Shania's arms. She struggled to hold him up, but his weight was too much. He slumped to the ground. Before she realized what had happened, someone grabbed her arm.

"You shouldn't be out here this late

what with that spook runnin' 'round, Miss Shania."

Dustin Harlow gripped her arm, a rifle in his free hand. Instantly she realized the foreman had snuck up on them and hit Jim in the back of the head with the rifle butt. A burst of hate exploded inside her, overshadowed only by her concern for Jim. She struggled to pull free, unsuccessful. "Let me go!" she shouted. "He might be hurt!"

"He'll be fine, missy, don't you worry none. Didn't hit him that hard." As if in response Jim Silverbird stirred, groaning.

"You sonofabitch!" Shania yelled, thumping a fist against Harlow's chest. "My father will hear about this!"

Harlow laughed and she didn't care for the note of cruelness in his tone. "Your father would likely give me a medal for it. 'Sides, that ain't no way to talk to your future husband."

"I'll never marry you! I swear to God I won't!"

The Indian boy suddenly gained his

feet and lunged at the foreman. Harlow let Shania free and swung his rifle to meet the charge. He got it partially up and the butt ricocheted off the boy's jaw with a solid *clack*.

Jim Silverbird staggered and Harlow re-adjusted his aim, burying the rifle butt in the youth's belly. The boy collapsed, gasping, squirming on the ground. Shania screamed, throwing herself at Harlow, hitting him over and over. The blows had no apparent effect. The foreman grabbed her, spun her around.

"Come along, Miss Shania. It's due time you should be getting yourself to bed. Don't worry none about the Injun, he'll live. They always do."

"You bastard!" she screamed, fury in her eyes. She took another swing at the foreman but he easily brushed it away. She struggled and kicked and cussed as he dragged her away from the creek.

★ ★ ★

Luke Banner tensed when he heard the yell. The shout broke the silence and he halted, listening intently. Forester's daughter. Waiting, he decided it hadn't been a yell of terror or fear; it was fury. He reckoned Shania Forester had just discovered Harlow following her.

In motion again, Banner stepped up his pace. While he figured the situation would not be critical, he went forward with speed and caution. You could never tell how folks would react in domestic situations; sometimes they wound up more dangerous than the hardcases.

More yells came from Shania Forester, followed by words he hadn't heard out of a lady since he'd been in a bar in El Paso. Crouching as he circled into the creek, he spotted the foreman half-carrying half-dragging the woman in the direction of the main house.

Banner pondered the situation: Harlow was taking her back to the ranch against her will, but it was probably for her own good. The foreman would want to protect her against the spook killing cattlemen. Obviously Shania didn't share his concern and she impressed Banner as a strong-willed woman with a mind of her own. He considered stopping the foreman, whom he noticed carried a Winchester, but that might present a problem. The foreman might be hot-headed enough to take a shot at him and Banner reckoned that would force him into the no-compromise situation of having to defend himself. It would complicate things more than he needed right now. Shania, angry as a hornet, would be safe enough, though when they reached the ranch she would likely catch all hell from her father for sneaking out.

For the time being, Banner checked his urge to interfere. Unless Harlow somehow tied into the case, Banner would let him be. Crouched, watching, he waited until they got half-way to the house before resuming his course. Banner couldn't return to the house for the present. If he did, Harlow would realize he'd been dogged and that would make him cautious in the future. Banner preferred to keep him off guard.

Reaching the creek, he paused. A sound caught his attention, one he couldn't quite pinpoint at first.

A groan. That's what it was. He surveyed the area, picking out the prone form of a man in the moonlight. Going to him, he stooped and turned the man on to his back. The fellow was young, dark-complexioned and Banner spotted blood leaking from the corner of his mouth. He struggled to sit up but Banner held him down. He couldn't be sure of the extent of the man's injuries.

"Easy, son," he said in a comforting voice. "Give it a moment and you'll be fine." Banner pulled loose the bandanna from around his neck and handed it to the boy. He accepted it and wiped the blood from his mouth. "You try to stand too soon and you'll find your world spinning. Take it from an old cuss who's had it happen a time or two."

The youth gazed up at him and Banner saw he was Indian, at least partially. He picked out the subtle indications of a mix, most likely white, in his features.

"Who the hell're you?" The youth's tone came challenging, angry, and Banner put things together. He knew why Shania Forester had snuck out of the house: she had come to meet this man.

"Name's Luke Banner. Yours?"

"Jim Silverbird. Got me a small spread yonder." He pointed, indicating a spot beyond the arroyo that split the land a mile or more distant. "Where you come from?"

"Everywhere." Banner's voice held a hint of sarcasm. "But for the moment I'm with the Circle H."

The youth grunted. "You an Indian-hater, too?"

He smiled, trying to put the boy at ease. "Not 'less I can pan some of the Sioux blood outa my veins."

The youth relaxed, a measure of

83

tenseness dissolving from his face. "What are you doin' at the Forester place, then?"

"Forester hired me to find a killer."

A look of panic struck the youth's face and he fought to gain his feet. Banner pushed him back, no easy feat considering the boy was strong as an ox. "Hold on, son, told ya you'd best sit a spell."

"I can't! Harlow's got Shania and I have — "

Banner shook his head. "Don't you worry none about that. He took her back to the ranch. She's fine, but likely'll get a scoldin' from her father."

Jim Silverbird eyed Banner, apparently taking his word for it, and calmed.

"Wanna tell me what happened?" Banner, waiting a few moments, helped Silverbird to his feet.

"Harlow hit me with a rifle butt."

Banner's eyes narrowed. "Why?" He could guess but he wanted to hear it from the boy.

"Shania wants to marry me but her

father won't hear of it."

"Any reason?"

"I'm part Indian, Mr Banner. Forester hates 'em and he ain't makin' no exceptions for half-breeds."

"And Harlow has it in his mind to get hitched to Shania?"

Silverbird nodded. "That's the whole of it, no buts. Her father wants that, too."

Banner understood. That was the reason for Shania's anger towards Harlow. She was in love with another man — a man her father did not approve of.

Banner let a thin smile touch his lips. "From the looks of things, I'd say she ain't got her mind goin' that direction."

Silverbird shook his head, which he appeared to regret immediately. He pressed his hands to his temples. "You're right 'bout that head spinnin', Mr Banner."

"We best get you back home," said Banner, noting the boy's wobbly condition. Silverbird made no effort to resist as Banner guided him towards the arroyo.

An hour later they sat in the parlor of the boy's modest plank home. The room was simple with solid furniture. Comfortable, Banner would have called it and he much preferred it to Forester's place. He took the liberty of building a fire while the 'breed brought out a bottle of Orchard whiskey, pouring two glasses.

"Had it brought to me by a friend in Indian Territory." Silverbird handed Banner a glass. "Beats the hell out of that snake-water whiskey the saloon serves."

Banner settled himself into a comfortable chair and took a swig. It burned smoothly all the way down, just the way he liked, and glowed in his belly.

"Ever been married, Mr Banner?" the youth asked, as he sat on the arm of the sofa. He cast Banner a solid steady gaze that bespoke character — a refreshing change from the likes Banner had encountered at the Circle H. He took an instant liking to him. Shania Forester could do worse than marry Jim Silverbird, he reckoned. From the looks of things the boy was honest and hardworking, free of the imposing self-importance that stuck like nettles to men such as Forester or the hard-edged manner of Harlow.

A distant look filtered into Banner's eyes as he thought over the boy's question. A woman's face entered his mind and he felt an ache in his heart. *Jamie* . . .

He had come so close. So close. But that was the past. He refused to dwell on it now.

"Can't say as I've had the pleasure."

Silverbird eyed him and Banner knew some of his pain had slipped on to his face. He rarely let that happen.

"Ever been close?"

His lips drew into a tight line and he hesitated. "Once, but it was long time ago."

"What happened, if you don't mind me askin'?"

Banner shrugged and downed the rest of his whiskey. He set the glass on the table.

"She . . . died." His voice chilled, thoughts going distant.

The youth's head lowered. "I'm sorry . . . didn't mean to pry."

Banner waved it off. "Don't let it trouble you, son. Just a bad piece of luck, is all. Happens to the best of men and I certainly ain't that." Banner knew his flippant tone didn't conceal the pain in his voice. He still dreamt of her, tortured by a nightmare that saw the same old scene played out over and over — her death. The feeling of loss never went away, never lessened. It just was and he could do damn little about it.

Silverbird changed the subject and Banner was thankful. "I love Shania, Mr Banner. With all my heart. And I'll do my best to see to it she has a good life."

Banner nodded. "I can see that plain as day. But her father ain't the type to let a grudge die, if I read him right."

Jim Silverbird nodded. "You read him right, surely you do. He won't let a grudge die, but he understands respect. Could say he's almost Indian in that way, though he'd soon enough put a hole in me if he heard me say it."

Banner chuckled. "Reckon you're right. But few men can get that from him. He's like a big ol' cock rooster when it comes to that, and he ain't likely to let you into the hen house without a fight."

"Got no desire to fight him, Mr Banner. Just want my due. I know I ain't got no obligation to him, but I want what's best for Shania and separating her from her father isn't it, if it can possibly be helped."

Banner smiled. "You got a good head on your shoulders, son, and I reckon you're right. But you got an uphill trail, that's for damn sure."

"You said Forester hired you to find

a killer . . . " The boy eyed Banner. "Stiller and Merton's?"

Banner nodded. "Know much about them?"

Jim Silverbird shrugged. "A little. Know they were friends with Forester and part of the Forester Cattlemen's Association. That's the extent of it. They never paid me much mind, which was just fine in my view."

"Any reason they might be killed?"

The boy thought it over, shook his head. "None that I can figure. Far as I know they were straight enough."

Contemplatively, Banner ran a finger over his upper lip. "I'm left kind of buffaloed by it. Usually men have a motive for killin', money, women, you name it."

Silverbird shook his head. "They all got money, more than they need. They got their agreement to live in peace in the Panhandle and help each other if need be. No women at stake, neither. They're all bachelors or widowers and spend their oats in the saloon."

"What about this spook?"

Jim laughed. "Indian legends are full of spooks, Mr Banner, but I can't claim to abide by such. Hell, maybe it's ol' Bob Diller come back way he said he would."

Banner straightened in the chair. "What do you mean?"

"Forester didn't tell you about it?"

"Forester ain't the most forthcoming of men. I got the feelin' he was leavin' something out."

A knowing look crossed the 'breed's face. "Reckon I can see why he might not say anything, too."

Banner settled back. "Who's this Diller?"

Silverbird took a swig of the Orchard and set his glass on the table next to the sofa. "He was a local. 'Bout six months back some steers turned up missin'. Ranchers went wild wantin' to put a stop to the rustlin'. They took after Diller 'cause the sheriff said he found some evidence."

"You don't believe he did?"

91

Jim laughed, then his face turned serious. "Stay away from Franklin, Mr Banner. He ain't one to be trifled with. He gets it in for you things could get mighty rough. Rumor has it folks got a habit of turnin' up dead when they get on his bad side."

Banner thought about it, then asked, "What happened to Diller?"

A grim look welded on to Silverbird's face. "Hanged him out by the creek."

"That the end of it?"

"No, he made a threat before he went, said he'd come back and get even, clean some clocks around here. Some say it was his spook that got Stiller and Merton."

Banner's eyebrows raised. "Hard to cotton to, but now I know what Forester was hidin', anyway."

"I gather the ranchers ain't so proud of what they done."

"Why not? They hung a rustler."

"Maybe." Jim shook his head. "But most folks don't think so. You go to the saloon in October Creek and you'll hear the talk. Diller's brother starts it. He was at the hangin' and spread it around about Bob's last words. You can bet he'll be spreadin' it sure after last night and blamin' it on the spook. Lucky if he doesn't get himself killed . . . "

"By who? The sheriff?"

Silverbird nodded. "He don't care none for anyone criticizing his decisions."

"What about you? You think Diller was guilty?"

"No, I don't."

"Why?"

"'Cause it's still happening, Mr Banner. Steers are still disappearing."

Banner's forehead crinkled. "Forester didn't mention anything about rustlin'."

"Oh, not a one would admit it, 'cept for Merton, who let slip at the last meeting some of his stock had 'wandered'. Guess he was feelin' the guiltiest."

"The others?"

"I got a feeling they all been losin' stock, though in small amounts."

"You?"

Silverbird nodded. "Yep. Lost me a few, but I keep a pretty tight watch and don't have as many head, so I'd notice quicker."

Banner thought it over. It still made damn little sense. A man falsely hanged for rustling, vowing to seek revenge, and now a spook carrying it out. He wondered why Forester bothered to hide the fact, unless he was just plumb scared or worried about being accused of hangin' an innocent man.

"I best be gettin' back." Banner stood, offering a hand. "Thank you kindly for the whiskey."

Silverbird shook, escorting him to the door. "Watch your back, Mr Banner. I know these men; they don't play around. Any one of them took a notion to drive me from the Panhandle I'd be gone. Be sure they don't take that notion with you."

"Appreciate the concern, son. Ain't many who'd have the sand to tell me that." Banner smiled. "I've gone a long time takin' care of myself and when it's my time it's my time. I fully believe that. Until then, I just keep doin' what I do."

★ ★ ★

The main house was lit up like a beacon by the time Luke Banner returned to the Circle H. Walking into the parlor, he saw three people standing near the settee — Caleb and Shania Forester and Dustin Harlow. Judging from the tense set of their faces, they'd been arguing. He reckoned Shania had been having her fill of the old man's mind for the better part of two hours.

"Where the hell were you?" Forester snapped, gaze locking on Banner, anger showing in his eyes. Harlow glared, but said nothing.

Luke came further into the room, removing his hat. "Wasn't aware I had to account for all my time, Forester."

Forester's face reddened. "By hell you don't with what I'm payin' you! Shania could have been killed tonight while you were out gallivantin'."

Banner damn near laughed at the ridiculousness of the statement, but stifled it, knowing it would do little good to infuriate Forester any further at the moment.

"Oh, Father!" Shania gave him a disgusted look. "It was nothing of the sort!"

Forester's face went almost purple. "I won't stand for you sneakin' out to meet with that . . . that Injun!" The cattleman waved his hands in frustration. "He could be the goddamned killer for all we know!"

She blew out a frustrated sigh and her eyes narrowed. She jammed her fists into her hips. "You're being foolish! If you could see past your own hate you'd know that."

Forester's voice jumped a notch. "I'm being practical! You could have been killed by that spook if not for Dusty, here. You best realize that, young lady."

A slight grin oiled Harlow's lips.

Shania threw up her hands. "You're impossible! Do you know that? When are you going to let me make my own decisions?"

"When you can start makin' the right ones!"

"Ones that don't involve Indians, I suppose!"

"Damn right!"

Shania's lips drew into a tight line and she rolled her eyes. Banner saw the frustration and fury in her blue eyes. She'd been over and over it with her father and gotten nowhere. She spun and hurried up the stairs before Caleb Forester could do anything but sputter.

"Christamighty!" he blurted at last, slapping his thighs. "She's got more stubbornness than a corral full of asses!"

"I'm inclined to agree, Caleb. Just glad I found her before that killer did." Dusty tipped his hat to the older man and brushed past Banner, flashing the manhunter a cold look.

When they were alone, Forester peered at Banner and said, "She was out in the middle of the night meeting with that goddamn half-breed, can you imagine?"

Banner felt his temper rise but suppressed the urge to give Forester a piece of his mind. "Reckon she's old enough to make up her own mind."

"You reckon wrong, Banner. If she was she'd know what was good for her."

"And what *is* good for her?" A note of sarcasm laced his tone.

Forester gave Banner a cold glare. "It sure as hell ain't marryin' some pissant cattleboy with Injun blood!"

Banner shrugged. "She's got the right to marry who she wants, doesn't she?"

Forester stiffened, giving him a look meant to intimidate. "You being contrary, Mr Banner? I don't like contrary men."

Banner refused to back off. "Just askin' a question. Take it or leave it."

Forester grunted. "She'll marry

Harlow, that's all there is to it. Won't have me no half-breed grandchildren."

"You got something against Indians?" Banner asked bluntly.

"You're goddamn right!" Forester fumed. "My brother was killed by the Comanche! You should have seen what they done to his body. Cut it up right awful, they did. Hardly left me enough to bury. I never told Shania that, but I will if it comes down to it." Forester shook with rage. Banner studied him, seeing the pain in his eyes. He could well identify with the man's anger, hurt, though he couldn't condone his hate. He knew the lust for revenge, the direction of hate all too intimately. But he knew the difference between himself and Forester as well.

"Don't make 'em all bad," he said. "Way I hear tell, we done some things to them."

"What are you, Banner, bleedin'-heart Injun-lover? 'Course they're all bad!"

"No, I'm just a man like you. I got my likes and hates, but I know who to blame."

Forester peered at him a moment, as if not knowing what to make of the answer.

Banner changed the subject. He didn't care to get into a discussion of philosophies with Forester. The man was bull-headed and set in his ways. He saw no changing him. "Why didn't you tell me about Diller?"

Forester looked startled. "Where'd you hear that?"

Banner shrugged. "Ain't important. All that counts is I did. Why didn't you tell me?"

"Didn't see no point in it. It's over with."

"Is it?"

"Hell, of course it is! Diller's dead and deservedly so."

"But the rustlin' ain't over."

"You don't know that, Banner, and it don't matter a lick. Plains will always have rustlers long as it's got longhorns.

Ain't gonnna stop on account of one no-good gettin' his neck stretched."

"You're right about that, Forester," Banner said with little conviction. He didn't know Diller but he would make it a point to find out about him. "Just hope you didn't act too quick and hang an innocent man."

Forester's eyes hardened. "Sheriff had evidence to the fact."

"Did he?"

Forester looked slightly puzzled. "Who've you been talkin' to, Banner?"

"Like I said, ain't important."

"Don't seem to me like you got much right to tell me how to go about dispensin' justice, seeing as how you got yourself all decked out as judge and executioner."

"You've got a point. But I don't allow other men to do the tallyin'. The men I kill are damn sure guilty. You can't say as much about Diller."

Forester went silent and Banner saw a touch of guilt in his eyes. He turned, heading towards the stairs, weary of the conversation. There was nothing more to say.

"Where you going?" Forester asked, tone losing some of its brusqueness.

"To bed. I ain't slept in three days and it's catching up with me."

"You're lucky, Mr Banner."

"How's that?" Banner sensed a challenge in the man's voice.

"You're lucky you're the best at what you do or I'd fire you for the remarks you made."

"Then fire me." Banner went up the stairs.

5

AS the sun dipped below the horizon and the shadows turned to onyx, Luke Banner rode into October Creek in search of Johnny Diller.

October Creek, an isolated trading post, was scarcely more than a way station. Scattered adobes and a general store peppered its rag-tag layout; a few shops filled the spaces between. A place where cowhands, blistered and beaten from the day's work tending herd could indulge in the gamier pleasures life had to offer. October Creek featured many dubious enticements — whores, rigged gambling, whiskey powerful enough to burn the lining from a man's stomach, and a smattering of brawls, legal and not. The settlement boasted its fair share of murders and, all in all, October Creek served as a stepping stone to Hell. Luke Banner had seen a hundred like it scattered across the West. He wasn't proud of the fact, but not exactly ashamed of it, either.

At the moment that little concerned him. He had it in mind to talk to the boy, discover whether there was more to the story of the hanging than Forester let on. Silverbird said the youth spent his nights shooting off his mouth in the saloon, so that seemed like the place to start.

The saloon was the largest building in the town, located just a short piece from the sheriff's office. As Banner eyed the office, Silverbird's warning flashed through his mind. He reckoned it'd be best to avoid the lawman if possible. He had run across the sheriff's type before, had even buried a few. Men who dispensed their personal brand of law, and dipped a hand into any number of the questionable pockets, taking a goodly percentage of the profits and offering 'protection' for a hefty sum. Dissenters were quickly silenced, often permanently.

It disgusted Banner, who considered such men no better than the hardcases he tracked — worse, in fact, because they set themselves up as trustworthy and took advantage of innocent folk. He felt a small measure of satisfaction every time he put a bullet in one, but he wasn't here for that. He was here to find a spook.

Banner sat his horse in front of the saloon. He crossed the boardwalk and pushed through the batwings into a raucous din of shouts and whoops and tinkling piano keys. A thick Durham and cigar fog hung in the air. Men, mostly cowhands, clustered around the dozen or so tables, drawing cards and cursing their hands; bucking the tiger or rolling chuck-a-luck dice. Saloon gals with kewpie-doll faces plied their dubious trade by hanging on to winners and snubbing losers. Paintings of nude women in unladylike poses adorned the walls and an array of sparkling glasses and mugs dangled from hooks. A coating of clumpy sawdust lay on the grimy floor.

Banner gave a thin smile and threaded his way through the sea of tables and patrons to the bar. Removing his hat, he set it on the counter. The barkeep, a husky gent, gave him the once-over, apparently deciding he looked acceptable.

"What's your poison, gent?" the 'keep asked. From his looks, Banner judged the 'keep could be rough on those he didn't cotton to.

Banner grinned, attempting to put the fellow at ease. "Got any bourbon?"

The 'keep bellowed a laugh. "Got one bottomless bottle and it's filled to the brim with rotgut."

"Well, by damn, rotgut it is!" The manhunter thumped a fist on the counter, adopting an air of joviality. The more he fitted in the better his chances of getting what he came for.

"Damn straight you will!" The 'keep flashed a missing-tooth grin and poured the whiskey. Banner flipped a silver dollar on to the counter.

The 'keep greedily snatched it up. "You're new here, ain't you?"

He nodded, glancing left then right at the men sitting to either side of him. He debated making up a song and dance, but decided against it. Maybe this one time he could use his unwanted reputation to his benefit.

"Yep, shorely am. Name's Banner."

The 'keep looked startled. "Luke Banner?"

"One and only." A twinge of unease stabbed his belly.

"Well, hell's bells! What in tarnation's a man like you doin' in these parts?" The 'keep showed obvious respect and a small dose of fear; Banner knew he had him.

"Lookin' for a spook, I reckon."

"Yeah?" The 'keep's brow crinkled.

He took a swig of his whiskey, probably the worst he'd ever tasted. "Lookin' for that hobgoblin that killed them ranchers."

The 'keep's lips drew into a tight line. "You got more balls than me, mister. If I came 'cross that *hombre* I'd be lookin' for a place to bury myself."

Banner chuckled. "Ain't worried none about no spook. It's the real men you gotta watch."

"Lookin' for any real men in particular?" asked the 'keep, taking Banner's lead.

"Damn straight. Came in here lookin' for Johnny Diller."

The 'keep's face went a shade whiter. "He done somethin', besides shootin' off his mouth, I mean?"

Banner shook his head. "Don't know, but I aim to have me a little parley with the fella and find out. Maybe he can help out. After all, was his brother who got hung."

The 'keep appeared somewhat worried. "You think the ghost of his brother has come back to git them men?"

Banner shrugged. "Told ye, don't

really cotton to the idea of spooks. From your answer, though, I'll take it you've seen him recently."

The 'keep appeared to think it over. "Say, if'n I tell you, you reckon I might get my name in one of them dime books I read about you?"

Banner groaned inwardly. "You never know with them no-good writers."

The 'keep grinned, relaxing, and nodded to his left. Banner followed his direction and peered at the young man half-slumped over the bartop.

"That him?" The manhunter looked back to the 'keep.

"He's quiet tonight 'cause he ain't started drinkin' in earnest yet."

"Much obliged." Banner slid off his stool and moved down three to sit beside Johnny Diller. Diller, a haggard expression on his face, glanced at him. Banner had seen the type before, though rarely so young. The boy's face was drawn, gaunt, with a sharp jawline and hollow cheeks. Dark circles rimmed his dull eyes and premature lines creased the corners of his mouth — the legacy of too much rotgut and too many nights of worry and loss. Banner knew the breed, all right. He was only a step away from that; only his lust for revenge 'saved' him.

"Who the hell are you?" the boy challenged.

"Like I told the 'keep, name's Banner and I'm here to find me a killer."

The boy let out a derisive laugh. "Them ranchers?"

"Yep. Ain't no reason they should be dead."

Diller laughed louder, a thing laced with spite. "Goddamn wrong there, mister. Them men deserved to die."

"Ain't what I heard, son. I heard they were right respectable cattlemen." While Banner put on a callous air, he felt sorry for the boy. Life just chewed some folks up and Diller was one of them. He had no future and likely would be sleeping with the worms in a short time. If some cowhand didn't stop his clock, rotgut would.

"You heard wrong, fella. They's killers, all of 'em."

"S'pose you tell me 'bout it." Banner motioned to the 'keep to bring the boy a fresh whiskey. The 'keep poured and set it in front of Diller, who snatched it up and downed it in one gulp.

"They killed my brother, Banner. Murdered him."

"I heard he was a rustler."

Diller's face went red and he slammed a fist on the counter. "Goddamn liars is what they is! Weren't no rustler and that sorry excuse for a lawman knowed it. Them cattle's still disappearin' and they ain't got my brother to blame it on no more." Fury showed in the boy's bloodshot eyes.

"How 'bout this spook, then?"

A vicious grin turned Diller's lips. "Hell, Bob's done come back way he said he would. He was a man of his word, Banner. That went with him to the grave, I reckon."

"A bit hard to swallow, ain't it?"

"Not if you knew Bob. He was as honest as they come. Didn't deserve what they done to him. Hope that spook kills 'em all, by hell I do. Serve 'em right."

Banner studied the youth, deciding he believed what he said. But was he lying all the same? Was he the killer? He certainly had reason and Banner had met many a killer who'd convinced himself of his own lies. Was that the case here? Diller was obviously a disturbed boy, in great pain; Banner knew that could cause a man to commit the unthinkable. He needed to know and that would take judging the reaction to his next question:

"Been doin' any killin' lately, Johnny?" His voice turned cold, penetrating.

Diller's face went livid. "What the hell call you got askin' me that?" He straightened on his stool, spittle flecking the corners of his mouth.

Banner held his ground. "Maybe you're the one who decided to make

Bob's threat come true."

"Why you sonofabitch!" Angry as a stuck bull Diller grabbed two handfuls of Banner's shirt and shook him. Banner was about to push him back when a hand grabbed the boy's shoulder and forced him back on to the barstool. Diller looked up, fear hitting his face. Banner's gaze shifted to the man standing beside them with a stern look on his face. The sheriff.

"What's the problem here, fellas?" The sheriff eyed Diller then Banner.

"Nothing, Sheriff," said Diller in a meek tone. "No problem at all."

"Just havin' us a friendly conversation," put in Banner, nodding.

"Didn't strike me as any too neighborly, fella."

Sizing up the sheriff immediately, he decided Silverbird's description had been accurate: the lawdog was no one to be trifled with. Behind the avuncular look and wire-rimmed glasses, Banner read an emptiness of soul and meanness of spirit. Franklin respected nothing but total control, domination over situation and men.

Banner kept his voice steady. "Friendly enough. Was just asking Diller here about the killin's."

Franklin eyed him, small eyes narrowing. "Yeah? And what gives you that right?"

A slight smile turned Banner's lips. "Caleb Forester hired me to find him. I aim to do just that."

"I ain't likely to cotton to that, Banner. If there's a killer to be found I'll do the findin'."

Banner's smile widened a notch. "You know my name?"

"Word gets around. Ain't much in its way in these parts and ain't much I don't find out about."

Banner held his ground. "I still got myself a job to do."

"Don't be doin' it here. I mean that. Your type ain't welcome in October Creek. I can't stop you while you're at Forester's 'less you do somethin' that rubs me wrong, but I don't wanna see you in town again."

"Didn't know better, I'd swear you were threatenin' me." Banner's temper rose but he held back. Now was no time to engage the sheriff in a confrontation. If that time came, Banner preferred they faced off alone.

"Get out and don't come back, manhunter. I won't make it any clearer than that."

Banner turned and downed the rest of his whiskey, then put on his hat. "Reckon I'll be on my way, then." He stood and Franklin eyed him.

"You got an attitude I don't like, Banner."

"Reckon that puts us on even ground." Banner gave the sheriff a curt smile and pushed past him. Franklin appeared on the verge of making a move but there was an air of posturing to it. He watched Banner thread his way to the door but didn't follow. Men like that were basically cowards at heart, and perhaps Banner had one more thing to thank that pulp writer for.

★ ★ ★

Five minutes after Luke Banner left the saloon, Sheriff Ben Franklin stepped outside and stared at the darkened street. He didn't like it, goddammit, not one bit. A man like Banner in October Creek meant trouble.

He had considered putting a slug in Banner, ending the problem right out of the gate, but a gnawing fear had stopped him. The man carried a reputation, lightning with a gun and merciless as old Lucifer himself. The fella was no cowhand or tinhorn gambler he could shoot in the back and sweep under a rug. The manhunter would be missed. That could bring a wagonload of unwanted attention. Banner wasn't an *hombre* known for letting men get the jump on him, either. Franklin had heard about men who had tried. More often than not those fellas wound up with third eyes. He had no wish to be one of them.

Franklin blew out a long sigh and

rubbed his chin. His brow crinkled. This was trouble, sure enough. Trouble they damn sure didn't need.

Franklin moved along the boardwalk, fishing paper and tobacco from his pocket and rolling a smoke. He drew in deep drags of Durham, sauntering as if he hadn't a care in the world. Reaching an alley at the end of the boardwalk, he lingered, making a point not to gaze in. He'd gotten used to these meetings; his boss had arranged it a half-hour ago, informing him that Banner had ridden into town in search of Diller. Franklin was ordered to interfere with the meeting, learn what he could.

A gruff voice came from the alley. "What happened?"

Franklin drew another drag from his cigarette. "He was in the saloon, askin' questions all right. Had Diller all flustered, too."

"Diller tell him anything?"

Franklin shrugged. "Probably nothin' 'cept about the ghost and his brother's hangin'."

117

A pregnant silence swelled and Franklin heard the din from the saloon.

"That might be good," the voice said at last.

"Reckon he suspects Diller?"

"Perhaps. What'd you tell Banner?"

"Told him to leave October Creek and not come back. Reckon that'll be the last of him." Franklin said it with an air of bravado. A smug expression oiled his lips.

A laugh sounded from the alley. The sheriff tensed, the expression dropping from his face. "What the hell you laughin' at?"

"He didn't take your advice."

"Whatta you mean?"

"Banner headed off towards Diller's cabin."

"Jesus H!" Franklin dropped his cigarette. "He's dangerous. We got too much at stake to have him snoopin' around. When he don't find nothin' at Diller's place, he might look elsewhere and leave the kid be."

"Don't worry, they'll all know it's Diller when the time comes. Besides, Banner's a dead man."

"Reckon I don't catch you?"

The unseen man grunted. "Had planned on gettin' me another rancher, but I think Luke Banner will be meetin' up with the spook first."

Franklin looked sceptical. "Hope you're right. We don't need his kinda trouble. I hear once he gets on a trail it's damn near the end."

"You worry too much, Franklin. By the time tonight's over Banner will be out of our way."

Franklin nodded but there was little conviction in it. "Reckon that's to be seen."

★ ★ ★

Luke Banner guided his bay around to the back of Johnny Diller's cabin. The place was dark, seemingly deserted. He had learned the location of Diller's homestead from Hinkley, the cowhand, before riding for October Creek. Of course the hand would go straight to Harlow with the information — who'd likely inform Forester — but Banner didn't rightly give a damn. Forester might well see no connection to the murders and Diller's hanging, but Banner didn't intend to overlook any bets.

Now was the time to search the place. With Diller tucked away in the saloon, the youth would be unlikely to stumble into Banner's search. Since the sheriff was with him, that took care of another factor.

Banner circled the dwelling and located an unlocked door. Inside the darkness was solid and he risked striking a lucifer. Locating a kerosene lamp, he set it aglow, turning it low to provide just enough light for searching.

The cabin's two rooms held little beyond a few rudimentary pieces of furniture and the basics, coffee pot, wood for the fireplace, scattered pans and utensils. Johnny Diller owned little and that would make the search easier.

He went through drawers and cabinets, most of which were virtually empty. He looked beneath furniture and padded down cushions and the worn mattress lying in a corner, making sure nothing was sewn into the linings. He found nothing and that didn't surprise him. The boy somehow didn't strike him as a killer. True, he had witnessed men kill for far less than revenge. Diller certainly showed no remorse or sympathy for the murdered men, but did that make him responsible for the deed? Was he loco? Diller was a man possessed by pain, loss, but in Banner's estimation far from crazy. The boy appeared genuinely indignant when accused of the killings, though what hardcase wasn't?

Diller wasn't a hardcase, he was just a boy; that was the difference. Banner knew people and he knew Johnny Diller was no criminal. While he couldn't let the youth off the hook completely, Johnny Diller's likelihood of guilt had dropped notches in his book.

His thoughts turned to the sheriff. With Franklin, Banner could take his dislike for Harlow and multiply it tenfold. His assessment was instant and harsh: Franklin was a genuine waste of a badge. He took advantage of his position, preyed on the weak. But did that relate to the case? Franklin, he felt sure, had a hand in many things illicit in October Creek — gambling, whores, possibly worse, but nothing about that was unusual for his type. Although he almost wished the sheriff would get in his way, bring about a confrontation, he had to let the matter drop. Franklin had no connection to the killings that he could see.

That left him with damn little trail to follow.

A sound caught his attention and at first he wasn't positive he had heard anything at all. Then a thought flashed through his mind and he knew what it was: a scuff, a boot dragging across a floorboard. He spun, but too late.

Something slammed into the side of his head. A coil of rope, bundled tight and hard as a hammer. A glancing blow, but enough to send him sprawling. He went down. Someone snatched his gun from its holster and hurled it across the room.

His head whirled and a muffled throbbing gonged at his temples. He struggled to move, gain control of his limbs, with little success. Through blurry eyes he glanced up, seeing something he couldn't rightly believe. A *thing* stood before him, a demon dressed in a black duster and black clothing. A man? The shape was right, but the face . . .

The thing wore a black Stetson pulled low over its bony brow. A grinning death's-head uttered a choppy laugh that came strained, raspy. At the neck, which looked to be flesh instead of bone, the burned-in impression of a rope showed. Light was poor and

Banner's gaze cloudy, but the image the thing presented was one of nightmare and peyote vision.

Spook or no, it was damned ugly and damned dangerous.

The thing laughed, a sound that cut right through him. Chilling, spectral, something from the grave.

The apparition moved forward, seeming to glide, though Banner clearly heard its steps. The sudden thought of what happened to those ranchers sobered him. He struggled to get to his feet, making it halfway. The figure sent a bootheel into his jaw. Banner saw it coming but was too stunned to avoid the blow. It clouted him backwards, and he landed with his sights fixed on the beamed ceiling. The ceiling gyrated as Banner lifted his head and tried to orient himself.

The ghost uncoiled the rope and Banner saw what it was — a noose! With a circular motion, the thing heaved the rope over a ceiling beam and secured the other end to a bureau leg. That accomplished, the apparition slid a chair beneath the noose and turned towards Banner.

Banner knew instantly he was slated to join those ranchers. And in that instant he knew he'd gotten on someone's bad side. Diller? The sheriff? Harlow? Who? He had no time to ponder it.

The ghost shoved his arms beneath Banner's. Dazed, the manhunter felt himself heaved on to the chair. He wrestled with his senses, struggling to get control of his limbs, but his body refused to respond.

The ghost uttered a hoarse laugh and forced him up, slipping the rope over his head.

"You don't belong messin' in things, Banner." The apparition's voice came raspy, unrecognizable. "You should have left well enough alone. Now it's too late."

The noose bit into his throat. In a moment he'd be swinging in the air, no chair beneath his feet.

The spook drew back a foot to kick the chair away.

Banner summoned what little strength he had left. His head still spun and his eyes watered, noose choking him. He kicked out frantically, barely keeping his balance on the chair.

His bootheel caught the thing square in the chest and sent it backward. He nearly stumbled off the chair, but managed to keep his balance. Prying the noose from his neck he slid it over his head.

The spook, recovered, charged him. It ploughed straight into Banner and they toppled backwards over the chair.

Banner hit the floor with a bone-jarring thud that snapped his head clear. He got off a limp punch to the thing's face that had little effect.

The spook got both hands around Banner's throat and tried to throttle him. Gloved fingers dug deep into the flesh, cutting off all air. Banner sent both arms up in a knife thrust and snapped outward. He broke the hold, but barely, gasping for breath.

The spook was powerful, too powerful in Banner's weakened condition, but inexperienced in fighting technique.

Banner thrust a knee into the spook's middle as it drew back for another assault. The ghost went backward and rolled, quickly regaining its feet.

Banner struggled to his hands and knees, bracing himself for further attack, but none came. His gaze lifted to see the apparition slipping out the back door.

Banner waited a few moments for his strength to return. He wanted to chase after the ghost but couldn't make his body respond to the command. He listened as footsteps receded rapidly into the distance. By the time he made his feet, still shaky, the spook was long gone.

Locating his Peacemaker, he blew out the lamp and went to the back door. He cursed himself for letting the thing get the jump on him. He simply hadn't expected it. Diller he felt sure would be occupied and how would the murderer know he was here? Had someone followed him? From the saloon? The Circle H? Deep in thought, he had been caught with his guard down when the thing snuck in the back quiet as a . . .

Ghost?

He suddenly hated that word, though it seemed to fit.

He stepped out into the night, making a quicky survey of the area, knowing it was useless. The spook had vanished.

A thought struck Banner and he dwelt on it. Why did the ghost leave its job undone? He was caught dead, stunned and unable to do more than a passing job of defending himself. The spook had every advantage. Why had it left? Noise? In a town like October Creek, no one would care. Folks were used to scuffles, and worse.

Was the spook afraid of Banner turning the tables and overpowering it? Again, Banner figured that wasn't the case. The spook damn near had him whupped.

Banner's hand drifted to the side of his head, feeling the abrasion and caked blood where the rope had connected. Maybe that was it: the spook wanted a clean hanging and though the law would do nothing about Banner's death, there was a risk men like Forester would call in reinforcements if they became suspicious they were dealing with something entirely earthly. That would make whatever the spook had in mind a hell of a lot more difficult.

As Banner withdrew his hand, he spotted something on the back of his knuckles. He had hit the spook's face and where his hand had connected lay a white smear. He drew a deep breath, rubbed at it, getting most of it off. Spook? Or merely a man? Had the apparition noticed the white smear on Banner's knuckles? Banner felt sure his explanation for the ghost's hasty departure was accurate. The spook wanted things clean and Banner had made that impossible. By fleeing it would be Banner's word alone — no proof.

A bit unsteady, Banner went to his bay and mounted. He'd keep his conclusions to himself, he decided, as he rode in the direction of the Circle H. But in his own mind, at least one thing was confirmed: he was dealing with the same kind of rattlesnake he always dealt with: a snake called man.

6

"**Y**OU look like hell!" said Caleb Forester as Luke Banner entered the parlor. He had ridden back to the ranch half-dazed. The night air had refreshed him but his head still felt like a thumb caught in a cinch.

"Arent you going to ask me where I've been?" He doffed his hat and stepped deeper into the room.

Forester gave him an irritated look. "What happened?"

"Had me a little run-in with our spook."

Shock welded on to Forester's ruddy face and he scratched his head. "You ain't havin' a laugh at my expense, are you, Banner?"

The manhunter laughed without humor. "Wish I could say I was." He selected a comfortable chair and dropped into it, exhausted. "I rode into October Creek to question — "

"Johnny Diller," completed Forester. "I know; Harlow told me. Can't say I appreciate it much, either."

Banner cocked an eyebrow. "Harlow told you?"

"Got it direct from the 'hand you asked about Diller."

Banner nodded, a motion that required some effort. He owed the rancher no explanation but didn't see any harm in telling him. "Wanted to question him about those killin's. Figured if anybody had anything against the ranchers it would be him."

Forester looked thoughtful. "Never thought of that. Maybe Diller's carryin' out his brother's threat."

"He don't impress me as the killer type, though."

Forester's brow crinkled and he sighed. "Reckon he ain't, but he was right peeled the night we hanged his kin. Woulda killed any one of us to stop it and he sure as hell tried."

"Six months is a long time, enough to cool down some. Reckon if he wanted to kill you he might have started before now."

"Not if he wanted to let the rustlin' die down for a spell before startin' it up again. Maybe he was helpin' his brother."

Banner considered it, quickly discounting the notion. "Don't see it. I've run across many a rustler and on the whole they're a pretty slick bunch. Diller don't appear to have the means to pull it off. He's just a boy and strikes me as honest enough."

"You put that together from just one meetin'?"

Banner nodded. "I'm a decent judge of a man. Have to be in my line of work."

Forester harumphed. "'Cept where Injuns are concerned."

Banner let the remark go. "Can't say the same for your lawman."

"Franklin?" Forester's eyes narrowed. "Had me a run-in with him at the saloon. Didn't seem to like me talkin' with Diller. Told me in no uncertain terms to stay away from October Creek."

With a grunt, Forester went to a table and opened a humidor. He offered Banner a cigar, who refused, then puffed his own stogie to life. "Franklin's as useless as they come, but he did find out Diller was rustlin' those steers, so I guess that makes him all right in my book."

"I'm inclined to disagree with you, Forester. Don't think he'd be much above makin' somethin' stick on an innocent man."

The rancher's face reddened. "You sayin' Diller wasn't guilty? That we hanged an innocent man?"

Forester appeared plainly annoyed by the accusation and Banner felt a twinge of satisfaction. "Ain't sayin' nothing you haven't thought yourself. It is possible, 'specially in light of the recent rustlin'."

Forester plucked the cigar from his

mouth. "Where the hell'd you get that load of cowflop? Ain't been no rustlin'. Steers wander. Happens all the time."

Banner shrugged. "Bet you add up all the wanderin' on all the spreads, including Silverbird's, and you'll find lots of your longhorns have decided to take their hay and run."

"Silverbird!" Forester blew out a disgusted grunt. "That Injun's probably responsible for enough rustlin' of his own. You know how them Injuns are."

"I know Jim Silverbird's as honest and decent as they come. Had me a talk with him."

"You been doin' your share of gettin' around, haven't you, Banner? Maybe Franklin's right; you should stick closer to home."

"Doin' my job, is all."

"Stay away from Silverbird. I mean it. I didn't hire you for that. He's got nothin' to do with this."

"Ain't makin' you any promises, Forester. Don't know where this case will lead."

Forester stared at Banner a long moment, trying to impose his will, but Banner refused to avert his gaze. The tactic might well intimidate greenhorns, but against a seasoned manhunter it was useless.

"You said you had a run-in with the spook?" Forester asked at last, giving it up.

"Went to take me a look around Diller's homestead, see what I could turn up. The spook tried to do to me what he done to Stiller and Merton."

Forester looked incredulous. "And you're alive to tell about it?"

"Reckon it was my lucky night. Caught me by surprise, I have to admit. Damn near got me, too."

"He got away?"

Banner nodded. "Wish I could say otherwise. But it makes me suspicious he turned up while I was at Diller's."

"Then it was Diller!" Forester's face took on a look of triumph, a look that quickly faded as Banner spoke.

"Could have been, but I think Diller

was much too occupied with the rotgut in the saloon to bother with me. Could mean someone followed me. That leaves me with another question."

"Such as?"

"Who knows enough about what I'm doin' to want to stop me? There's you, Harlow, the 'hands here at the Circle H, Diller, the barkeep, and Franklin. Reckon I can rule out you and the barkeep."

"Don't forget Silverbird; I assume you told him?"

"Yep. But he wouldn't have known I was in town."

"Unless he happened to be there and saw you."

"Didn't see him, so I think that's stretchin' it."

Forester grumbled. "Injuns are damned sneaky when they wanna be."

Banner chuckled and eyed the rancher. "I reckon Silverbird would make you a right fine son-in-law."

"Jesus H!" Forester yelled. "Shania's got a future, Banner, and it ain't with no 'breed! She'll marry Harlow, by God, I'll make sure of that!"

"You can't tell her who to love."

"The hell I can't! She's my daughter and I want what's best for her. That's Harlow in my book."

A thin smile filtered on to Banner's lips. "Maybe she'd like to make up her own mind on that account."

"She's young and impetuous. She don't know what she wants yet."

"Seems to have a pretty good head on her shoulders. Maybe you should give her a bit more credit."

Forester's voice jumped a notch. "This is none of your business, frankly. I hired you to catch a spook, not dispense family advice."

Banner nodded. He would let the subject drop. "True, but this ain't no spook we're after."

"You said you met it?"

"Did. But I hit it and it was damn solid." Banner glanced at his knuckles, eyeing the spot where he had rubbed off the smear of white.

Forester shook his head and blew out a long sigh. "Rightly don't give a diddly damn what it is. Just get it before it kills again."

Banner stood and went to the window, gazing out into the night. "That's what I aim to do, 'less something happens in the meantime . . . "

★ ★ ★

Cale Hadley, dressed in long-johns and toting a Winchester, crept from the main house of his Bar Double L spread to the livery. A sound had plucked him from a nightmare-wrought slumber, a sound chilling and spectral: a laugh, shivering across the still, moonlit night. A laugh like the cackle of demons. Half-asleep, he wondered whether he'd heard it at all, about to dismiss it as a dream when it sounded again. No dream, though Godamighty his dreams were filled with spooks and things that walked the night since the murders of Stiller and Merton.

Some whispered Diller had returned from the dead to seek vengeance. Hadley refused to believe that, though he admitted the notion bled into his nightmares. He recollected the night they hung Diller as clearly as if it had been yesterday. He hadn't taken a complete night's sleep for two months after the hanging. Now the nightmares were back, because Diller's kin was shootin' off his damn fool mouth at the saloon and one of Hadley's men had overheard it and brought it to his attention.

"Spooks, hell," he muttered. "No such thing!"

But the laugh.

He shuddered, stepping on to a cool patch of grass. A filament mist, embroidered with silver threads of moonlight, wisped along the ground; he felt its chill moist kiss on his bare feet. He gazed up at the starry sky, the alabaster moon. Damn, nights like this gave him pause, especially with that killer running around. Sometimes he hated the loneliness of the Plains, the endlessness of the land. A body could easily imagine all manner of things, shadows that seemed alive, ghosts scampering with the fog.

Maybe you're next . . .

The thought startled him more than he dared admit. That's why when he heard the laugh he had jammed a full load into his Winchester and come out into the night. He'd damn sure fill any spook he happened across full of holes.

No such thing as a spook.

Couldn't be.

He wished he could make himself believe it.

He reached the livery, halting, hands bleached as he clenched the rifle tighter and stared at the huge double doors. One was open. That wasn't right. Not right at all. He felt positive the doors had been secured earlier.

Why was it open?

The question boogered him. It didn't belong open and by God he swore that laugh had come from this direction.

He shuddered again.

Going forward, he kept the Winchester level and well in front of him. Spook or no spook, whoever had made that laugh and opened the livery door was in for a bad night for frightening him so.

Hadley paused at the opening, peering into the dark maw of the livery. The scent of leather and dung and hay reached his nostrils. Moonlight sliced across the hay-strewn dirt aisle and he heard horses nicker. They sounded disturbed, unsettled.

"Who's there?" he asked, heart starting to bang.

No answer.

Another shudder. The Winchester started to shake. "I said, who's there? Come on out or you'll be leakin' from your vitals!"

One of the horses gave a worried neigh. Hadley clenched his teeth so tight muscles stood out like whitened marbles on either cheek. He edged through the opening, halting just inside the door and waiting for his eyes to adjust to the gloom.

Something caught his attention: one of the horses stood in the centre of the livery, out of its stall.

"What the hell?" He took a few steps closer to the animal, cocking his head. "Chester?" The sorrel lifted his head in a jerky movement. "What the hell you doin' out of your — "

Something collided with the back of Hadley's head, something with all the softness of an anvil. The Winchester flew from his grasp and he stumbled forward, falling against the horse. He managed to keep his feet, gripping handfuls of the horse's mane. His head whirled and his legs threatened to abandon him.

A chilling laugh ululated from the darkness. He tried to turn but something hit him again, this time connecting with the side of the face. The blow shattered his cheekbone and blood blew in a spray from his mouth.

Hadley collapsed as if his legs had

been chopped from beneath him. Half-conscious, he hit the dirt face first, aware of someone moving above him. Arms jammed beneath his own, heaving, propping him against the horse, then hoisting him on to the animal's back.

With a terrifying burst of realization, his vision snapped clear and his gaze lifted. Above him dangled a noose.

"Nooo," he muttered. The laugh sounded again, chilling, mocking. Turning his head, Hadley saw the ghastly thing standing beside the horse. Outlined in cold moonlight, it appeared to be a spectre from the blackest western night. Its skull face glimmered with captured moonbeam and its death's-head grin sent a shock of terror through his being.

"Christamighty . . . " Blood ran from his mouth.

"Time to pay your due, Hadley," the thing said in an eerie voice that Hadley swore belonged to the Devil.

The spook reached up and placed

the noose around the rancher's neck, tightening it.

"Please," Hadley tried to shake his head, "have mercy."

The spook laughed. "Why? You had none on me . . . "

The ghost slapped the horse on the rump and the sorrel leaped forward . . .

★ ★ ★

You're getting soft . . .

Luke Banner fell into the huge feather bed, exhausted. His head banged and his bones ached. The encounter with the spook had left him battered and drained. He chastised himself for being caught off guard, knowing full well the mistake had nearly cost him his life. Was he losing his touch? They said that happened to manhunters, usually all at once. Reflexes slowed, just a hair at first, degrading by fractions, until some faster gun beat him to the draw. If that failed to happen, a shooter just woke up one morning with the stiffness in his fingers and the heaviness in his soul. Death, now assured, usually came swift and sudden, delivered from behind or while asleep by some faceless enemy, a loose end from the past. Too many hardcases recollected Luke Banner.

But that would be a blessing, because he knew he'd never be able to live with the ghosts.

Her ghost.

He couldn't afford another mistake. Slowing or not, he would not allow himself that luxury. Hunches and a few shreds of evidence were linking in his mind, though not enough to accuse anyone yet. He still had a little matter of motive, and that left him with a big gap in his figuring. The case was more than simple ghostly vengeance; there had to be some buried reason. The spook hangings were merely a cover, an imaginative ploy by some clever, if skewed, mind. Suspicious cowhands and ranchers might be taken in by such nonsense, but Banner believed in the evil of men, the evil that made one man hate another enough to kill for money or misguided belief. Evil in its purest form. That was the evil that existed in the Panhandle, not some spook of the night.

Exhaustion overtaking him, Luke Banner drifted into a restless slumber. Images laced his dreams, things he prayed he'd forget. He never did. They were always there, waiting.

The duplicity of Luke Banner, the man he used to be and was now, bundled together yet separated, tortured him. Two men; one hidden, locked away, the man who had loved and desired a life of happiness and peace; the other a killer, a man bitter and twisted by his lust for vengeance against those who had taken Jamie from him.

He couldn't stop the dream. When it came it came like Colorado thunder, and he was captured by the storm.

She was there, haloed in the sunlight of those past times, the warm light of the angels bathing her, glowing in her golden hair.

Dreams. That's what it boiled down to, plain and simple. Dreams of starting their life together, building a fine home and cattle business up Wyoming way. A few steers and some blacksmithing. He'd laid it all out and nothing could get in his way.

"I love you, Banner," Jamie said, hair glossed with sunlight as they stepped from their saddles by a stream that meandered through the tract of land he planned for their homestead.

"It's all here for us, isn't it?" Luke swept his hand across the vista of virgin land. Rich and fertile, it went on as far as the eye could see. "This is what we always wanted."

She went to him, taking his hand, and he pulled her into his arms. She felt so comfortable there, a part of him, and in a month they would marry. Luke Banner would lead the life he always wanted, longed for. A dream, a wonderful sunlit dream.

A bloodstained dream.

A nightmare.

A commotion sounded behind them and he lifted his head to see two men emerging from the forest that skirted the stream. Both looked to be hardcases, Smith & Wessons at their hips, a dull coldness glinting in their eyes. A vague panic invaded in his mind.

"Well, lookee here," one of them said, drawing his gun. "Ain't this a right purdy sight to behold?"

"Reckon you got that right, Jeb," the shorter man said, grinning with tobacco stained teeth.

With a sweep of his hand, Luke forced Jamie behind him. "What do you want? I own this land. Please leave."

The man named Jeb chuckled and his gaze lingered on Jamie longer than Luke felt comfortable with. "Don't own it yet. Fact is, our boss wants this land. We're here to see that he gets it."

Luke bristled. "I put my bid in fair and square. Ain't my fault your boss couldn't match it."

"You bid too high, Banner. That's the problem. He ain't about to pay that price when he can get it cheaper."

"You know who I am?"

"Surely do," said Jeb.

"Who are you working for?"

"Ain't sayin', just that he had the second highest bid and that's enough."

Banner stiffened. "Easy enough to find out. When I do I'll see to it the sheriff puts a stop to this kind of outrage."

"You ain't gonna get the chance, Banner," said the shorter man, going for his gun while Jeb brought his to aim.

Banner knew instantly they meant to kill them both. He couldn't let that happen. He had always been fast with a gun and the one at his hip was loaded and ready in case they encountered snakes or predators. But could he draw in time to stop Jeb from killing him first?

A split second of decision — not

enough time. Before he could draw he would be dead.

Without thought, he took the only alternative. He hurled himself at Jeb, knowing he had to save Jamie at any cost, even that of his own life.

The distance between them was less than five feet and the leap took him clear into Jeb. They went backwards. Both hit the ground hard and the wind burst from Banner's lungs. Jeb's gun went off. The bullet tore a welt across Banner's side, but did no real damage.

To him.

A scream ripped out behind him, though at first he couldn't see why. He fought with the hardcase, rolling, managing to get a hand on the Smith & Wesson. Forcing it around, he triggered a shot. The man went limp, blood gouting from a gaping wound in his chest.

By that time, the second man had his gun out and was drawing a bead on Luke's head. He rolled, pulling Jeb's lifeless form over him as a shield.

The hardcase fired. The slug ploughed into the dead man's back. The impact jolted Banner, but he jerked his captured gun up and squeezed the trigger.

The second hardcase took a stuttering step backward and went down flat on his back. Banner rolled the body off of him and gained his feet.

The hardcase wasn't dead. He pushed himself into a sitting position, hand still locked to his gun.

Banner triggered another shot. The bullet shattered the hardcase's forehead and sent a spray of brains and blood and bone out the back of his head. He was dead before he hit the ground.

Banner breathed a sigh of relief that lasted only an instant. For when he looked over to Jamie he realized why she had screamed. He stood frozen, in horror, in grief. She lay on the ground, arm outstretched, fingers curled. Her eyes glared sightlessly upward.

Shaking off the spell, he ran to

her, kneeling and pulling her close. She was gone, though he refused to believe it. For the first and only time in his life Luke Banner felt tears leak down his face. He screamed up at the unforgiving sky, swearing at a God who seemed powerless, uncaring, who had let her life be snuffed out without a thought. A callous God who fashioned men like the two lying dead a few feet away.

In the days after Jamie's funeral he found his emotions quickly receding, tucking themselves away in the dark corners of his mind. Replaced by a cold seething fury, an icy lust for vengeance. He was no longer a man really; he couldn't be if he hoped to survive. Grief was too powerful, love too strong. He spent a day or two considering putting the business end of his Peacemaker into his mouth and pulling the trigger, making the pain vanish forever. But something took over, some soulless thing inside, turning him into something almost inhuman. He reached a decision: men like the hardcases who had killed his Jamie deserved to die. Not him. They wanted to die. *Craved* it. And he would give them what they wanted.

It hadn't taken long to hone his tracking abilities, shave fractions of seconds from his draw speed. They had always been there, though he hadn't known why until now. Gifts, a trivial compensation for dread loss, but he would use them to strike down those who deserved it. Within a short time he discovered the man responsible for hiring those hardcases to steal the land from him. He tracked the rancher down, cornered him in the dead of night, forcing him to go for his gun. The man soon lay at the bottom of his well, a bullet between his eyes.

The men responsible for Jamie's death were gone, but satisfaction was fleeting, hungry. He gave up his option on the land and set out manhunting, never settling in any one place for too long, gaining a reputation as a fast gun and sure shot, a tracker extraordinaire. He developed contacts and dime novels filled pages on him. In time he became almost a mythical thing, a mechanism of vengeance, never satiated. Driven by inner fury and justice. He fashioned the Banner Detective Agency, leaving himself free to do the dirty work. The work of killing.

Luke Banner sat bolt upright in bed. A sound had snapped him from his nightmare and he was thankful for it. His heart stuttered and sweat streamed down his face. He sucked deep breaths, steadying himself and listening, waiting for the sound to come again, for a moment wondering if the spook he'd encountered earlier tonight had returned. But that wasn't it. The commotion was caused by Forester's raised voice from downstairs.

Banner swung his feet out of bed and quickly dressed. Going downstairs, he found Forester, Harlow, Shania and the sheriff gathered in the parlor.

Franklin gave him a corrosive glare, but said nothing.

Forester shook his head. "Appears you didn't move fast enough, Banner. There's been another killin'."

Luke's belly knotted. "Who?"

"Hadley. One of his men found him hangin' in his barn."

"Why are you here?" he asked Franklin, in no mood for small talk.

Franklin looked annoyed. "Figured Forester and the rest had a right to know."

Banner cocked an eyebrow. "Sure you just didn't want to put the fear of God into them?"

The sheriff's eyes narrowed and his face pinched. "What the hell's that s'posed to mean?"

Banner ignored the question. His gaze shifted to Harlow, whose clothes appeared fresh and whose face looked slightly drawn but alert. "You don't look like you've been to sleep yet, Harlow . . ."

Harlow's posture went rigid. "Don't

think I care much for your tone, Banner."

"Answer my question." He held the man's gaze.

Howard deflated some. "Was in town playin' poker till late. Just got in a while ago."

"Don't recollect seein' you while I was there."

"Got there late. Had business to finish."

"That a fact?" Banner turned to Forester before Harlow could retort. Forester was directing his attention at the sheriff.

"Well?" the rancher prodded the pudgy lawman, who appeared to be still seething over Banner's question.

"Well, what?" Franklin's tone had iced over.

"What are you going to do about this, Franklin? That's three men killed. We're all in danger."

Franklin's gaze darted to Harlow, Forester and Banner in turn. "Appears to me you took matters into your own hands, here, Caleb, for all the good it's done you."

Forester cussed. "He's at least had a tussle with the spook! You ain't done a goddamn thing but ride around tellin' folks about it."

A smirk oiled Franklin's lips as he looked at Banner. "Met the spook and you ain't dead? Almost a pity, ain't it?"

Banner considered laying the man out for the remark. Nerves raw, temper hair-triggered, it wouldn't take much. He suppressed the urge. There would be another day for that, but right then he made up his mind: warning or no, he intended to have himself a little parley with Franklin tomorrow. The spook attack left too many unanswered questions in his mind. The lawman was going to account for some.

"Hell," Forester interrupted, "that only leaves Sharpe and me for this damned hobgoblin to come after."

"'Less you count Harlow and me, as well as the deputy," put in the sheriff. "We were all present at the hangin'." The statement clearly rankled Forester.

Harlow shot Forester a glance, worry crossing his face. "And Diller."

"Reckon Diller ain't got much to fret on," the sheriff said, "if it's his brother's spook . . . ."

"This is gettin' us nowhere!" grumbled Forester, holding up a hand in a halting gesture. "I insist you do something, Franklin. You're the law here."

"What would you have me do? This spook ain't exactly presentin' an easy catch."

"Arrest Diller, then! He's got the motive!"

"On what grounds?" Franklin raised an eyebrow.

"I don't know — anything! Just do something." Forester let out a disgusted sigh and fell into a chair, looking plainly exhausted. Banner could understand why. Three of his fellow ranchers had been murdered and now the number was down to two, himself and Sharpe. Who would be next? Four others had been present at the hanging — Harlow, Franklin, a deputy and Johnny Diller — but Banner discounted the revenge theory and doubted those men were in any danger. He felt, despite the rancher's talk of arresting Diller, Forester knew it as well.

"I'll sleep on it, Forester," said Franklin. "That's the most I can promise." He tipped his hat to Shania and gave Banner a parting glare, then walked out. Harlow followed suit after making an effort to say goodnight to Shania, who predictably snubbed him. She went to her father and touched his shoulder, trying to comfort him. Banner peered at Forester, who glanced up.

"I'm not the type to bow to others, Banner," he said, tone weary. "Usually I take care of my own. But I'm askin' you, now: please find this spook and do away with it before it can harm my daughter."

Banner nodded, mustering sympathy

for the bull-headed rancher. "I'll give you my word on that. I won't let anything happen to her." He wondered suddenly why he had promised that, knowing full well the elusive spook could easily make a liar out of him. But the image of Jamie from his dream pushed into his mind and he reckoned he knew the answer: he had been powerless to stop her death, but he'd be damned if he'd let it happen again.

Going back to his room, he fell into bed, considering the night's events, the spook attack on himself and the death of another rancher. If he intended to keep his promise to Caleb Forester, he needed to act, even if it meant risking his own hide.

7

THE morning sun blazed in the cloudless sky, gilding the emerald sea. As Luke Banner, standing beside his bedroom window, peered out at the Plains, he wondered when the spook would strike again. The remainder of the night had passed dreamlessly, though the after-memory of Jamie left a longing the sight of the grasslands didn't ease. He could have lived this life, the life of a cattle rancher. A gruelling yet idyllic life of peace, for no amount of toil would have mattered as long as Jamie stood by his side. The loss saddened him; deep aching pain rose in his soul. Perhaps that's why he had stuck his nose where it didn't belong; he had no business mixing in the dispute between Silverbird, Shania and her father. While he felt positive Forester was misjudging the youth, letting his petty prejudices cloud his vision, it was not his fight. He identified with Forester's pain and hatred, inflicted by the loss of a brother, but he couldn't see blaming an entire race for the deeds of one.

Isn't that what you're doing?

He had to admit that in a way he was. The men he went after deserved to die — murderers, hardcases, bandits all. He could honestly argue he made the West a better place for decent folk; some would even believe him. They never glimpsed the demon of vengeance inside Luke Banner, the demon he kept hidden, chained, the demon who'd never leave until he wiped that feeling of helplessness, guilt from his blood-drenched soul.

In some perverted way that separated him from Forester — the focus of hate. Forester was haunted by an impotent hate, while Banner was possessed by a burning living vengeance. Some folks wouldn't see the dividing line, but he saw it; that's all that counted in his book.

He reckoned that Jim Silverbird and Shania Forester deserved the chance he never had; the chance to live.

For the time being that had to be as far as it went. He had said his piece and maybe he would say more if the opportunity presented itself, but today his focus needed to be on the killer. In his mind, the plan was cast — a ride to October Creek to bang a few woodpiles, see what slithered out. He had suspects, though few leads, and that's where he'd aim his attack. Franklin, who was known to be shady; Johnny Diller, though Banner had doubts there; even Harlow, no matter how unlikely, had to be considered. Banner ruled out the ranch 'hands and Forester, but would keep Silverbird on the active list. Damned unlikely, but he could see where the youth might develop a hatred for the ranchers.

However, real motive was still lacking for all except Diller. Yet he knew one had to be there. Men didn't kill for idle reasons, at least in their own minds. Revenge, hate, greed, jealousy — something powerful enough to drive a man to murder, in this case by elaborate means, and Banner would find it.

He turned from the window and headed downstairs, going out to the livery to saddle his bay. Stepping into the saddle, he rode for October Creek. Franklin had warned him to stay out of town, but two of his suspects were there, and that was enough motivation to make him ignore the sheriff's order. Fact was, the lawdog was first on his list. He could handle Franklin as long as he didn't turn his back on him. The move carried a certain risk: to rile the lawman meant sticking his hand in a rattlesnake hole. That was a chance he had to take.

As Banner rode, he sifted through what he knew of the lawman. Franklin had found (planted?) the evidence pointing to Bob Diller being a rustler. So? That meant little, unless the crime could be pinned on Franklin and he had needed a scapegoat. Possibly the lawman was just lazy, wanting to waste little time chasing down the real thief; or possibly he sought the notoriety bringing down the rustler might give him in the eyes of the ranchers.

Could Franklin be connected with the rustling? A possibility, but he had to admit the notion was tenuous without evidence to back it up.

His thoughts shifted to Johnny Diller, the second man on his itinerary. Franklin had interrupted them in the saloon last night and Banner intended to question the boy further. While he needed no thought as to Diller's motive, it made the case appear too pat; that always sounded a warning bell in his mind. Little in his line of work came easy and he doubted this case was any exception. The ghost had shown up at the boy's cabin. While Franklin or Forester would have taken that evidence as gospel — possibly even hang Diller on it, Banner had struck too many gold veins beneath the rust to accept things at face value.

October Creek appeared on the horizon and a twinge of apprehension pierced his belly. He smiled a thin smile. Good, it would keep him alert. He commonly felt that tingle of nerves when things started to brew on a case.

He rode into the settlement, drawing looks from folks meandering along the boardwalk, some drunk, doubled over hitch rails and emptying their stomachs on the dirt. Down the street, he saw a knock-down-drag-out, which the townsfolk cheerfully ignored. Shaking his head, he drew up in front of the sheriff's office and dismounted.

Franklin sat behind his desk, leaning back, feet up, playing a hand of poker with his deputy. As the door opened, he looked up, surprise mixing with a vicious look on his face.

"Goddammit, I thought I told you — " His feet thudded off the desk and he half-rose, hand going towards his gun.

He froze in mid-draw.

Banner's gun seemed to magically appear in his hand. In a blur of movement he drew, centring his aim on the sheriff's barrel chest. Franklin's gaze locked with his, averted. Banner's speed commanded his attention and respect. The deputy sat stone still, shock on his face.

Banner heeled the door shut behind him. "You got two ways to play this, Franklin: one way you sit your fat ass back in that chair and listen; other I give you a third eye." Franklin knew he meant business. The lawman ran his tongue over dry lips and sank into his chair, defeat and a healthy dose of fear in his eyes.

Banner slid the Peacemaker back into its holster. "Figured you'd be willin' to co-operate with a fellow lawman." With a glare, Banner pinned the deputy, who seemed at a loss at to what move to make next, to his chest.

"Thought I told you to stay out of October Creek?" Franklin's tone came icy, vaguely threatening.

Banner grinned. "Reckon I'm a mite hard of hearing."

"'Nother hole in your head might improve that."

"I'll be sure to keep that in mind, Sheriff. But for now I'm lookin' at tyin' up these spook killin's."

Franklin tensed. "What do you mean?"

"Whelp," Banner stepped further into the room, slinging a leg over the corner of the desk and resting a forearm across his knee. "I got me some notions about that spook."

"What kind of notions?" asked Franklin. Banner looked for any hint of guilt in the sheriff's eyes but saw none. The man was an expert poker player where hiding guilt was concerned; he'd had years of practice.

"Why, just who this spook might be."

Franklin cocked an eyebrow. "Who?"

Banner laughed. "Maybe you, Sheriff."

Franklin let out a guffaw but Banner

sensed more tension behind the laugh than there should have been. He wondered if he had hit on something. "Tarnation, Banner, you lost your goddamn mind! I got nothin' against those dead men. Fact is, I helped bring down their rustler."

"Some say you accused an innocent man."

"Who says, Johnny Diller? He's always shootin' his mouth about that. Never could accept the fact his brother was a thief, so it's only fittin' he'd be accusing us of wrong-doin'."

"There's others," Banner said, stretching it a bit.

"Name 'em, Banner." A dark look crossed Franklin's eyes and Banner knew to give him Silverbird's name would mean a wagonload of trouble for the youth.

"I'll just keep that to myself, Sheriff. Suffice it to say I got me a notion to believe them. You don't really strike me as the type to uphold the law 'less you got somethin' to gain from it."

Despite the accusation, Franklin relaxed a bit. "And what would I have to gain from killin' those ranchers? Tell me that, manhunter."

The sheriff had him on that point. He couldn't tie Franklin to rustling, let alone the killings. Franklin knew it as well.

"Can't rightly see as how you'd gain, but that don't mean the reason ain't there."

Franklin let out a grunt. "Then I suggest you get yourself some evidence 'fore you come in here accusin' me again. Next time you might not get the draw on me."

The threat was blatant and Banner knew he'd achieved his goal. He'd served Franklin notice, informed him he regarded him as a suspect. That might make him edgy if he had something to hide. He had played a hunch and the payoff was yet to be seen; he might draw a full house or a bust.

Banner edged off the desk and backed to the door. "I'll be in town

171

a spell longer. I suggest you stay in your office." The threat was delivered with the utmost confidence. Franklin nodded slowly.

"I'll let you have that this time, Banner. But it'd be healthier for all if you kept your business out at the ranch from now after."

Banner smiled thinly. "I'll be tyin' up my work there soon. After that you won't have to worry about me — 'less of course you do something that gets my attention."

Outside Banner sauntered along the street, leading his horse by the reins and mentally indexing his meeting with Franklin. A lawman like him proved easy and difficult to read at the same time. An obvious crook, but when it came to specifics a master at keeping his hands clean. Such men were hard to pin a charge on. They slipped through the hands of justice like a greased pig, though Banner, free from legal constraints, wouldn't hesitate to stop his clock if the opportunity presented itself. He felt confident Franklin wouldn't bother him for the moment, but the future would warrant caution. He'd riled the lawdog and you didn't go into a bear's den unless you had a Winchester loaded and ready. Franklin would bide his time until he could find a way to get even, and the manhunter would keep on the lookout for trumped-up charges. His suspicions aired, he might well end up sharing Bob Diller's fate.

He stopped outside the saloon and tethered his horse to the hitch rail. The man next on his list would likely be warming a stool at the bar, even at this early hour.

Banner shoved through the batwings. The place held few patrons, mostly tinhorns and would-be gamblers getting a step on the night's activities. A handful of bar doves lolled about, leaning on the counter, or gamblers' arms. Two cast him looks, obviously deciding he wasn't an easy mark and going back to their business.

He walked up to the bar and the 'keep gave him a raised eyebrow.

"Didn't think I'd be seein' you back here after the sheriff's warnin' the other night."

Banner shrugged. "The sheriff and me have an understandin', for the day, at least."

"Yeah? Franklin ain't usually one to make peace agreements."

"Reckon you just need the right Peacemaker . . . " Banner gave a cold smile.

"What's your poison?"

"There a choice?"

The 'keep grinned and poured a whiskey, sliding it before Banner. Banner downed it in one gulp. He thunked the glass on the bar and eyed the 'keep.

"I'm lookin' for Diller again. Sheriff interrupted me last time and I aim to finish my conversation."

The 'keep shrugged. "Can't help ya this time. Diller left just after the sheriff. Ain't seen him since."

"That unusual?"

"Who knows with him? Usually he's in here a hunnert times a day. He's probably sleepin' it off somewhere."

"Much obliged." Banner tipped his hat and slid off the stool. On the street, he contemplated the boy for a moment and decided to check Diller's cabin. A man like Diller shouldn't prove hard to track down, but a vague sense of something wrong rose in his mind. The feeling told him he wouldn't find Diller at the cabin or anywhere else.

The cabin was empty. The rope still hung from the ceiling, indicating Diller likely had never returned home last night. Odd, that. Where else would he go?

Next Banner made a cursory search of the settlement. He probed alleys and scoured the streets. It took him just over an hour to determine Johnny Diller was nowhere on the street.

Banner wondered if the lad had friends who might give him a bed, but discounted that possibility quickly. A man like Diller would have run plumb out of friends by now. Though young, he had turned into a ranting drunk and likely folks were sick of listening to his talk. That's why he spent so much time at the saloon. He'd traded companions for whiskey.

After the search of the town, Banner felt sure of the feeling in his gut. Something had happened to Johnny Diller. But what?

8

REACHING the Circle H compound, Banner drew up near the livery and dismounted, leading his horse towards the stable. He wondered how long it would take before something came of his talk with Franklin — assuming, of course, the man was involved. He felt impatient, but figured things would move faster when he hit the right suspect. From the attack by the spook, Banner knew the situation was already tense; now just to push it along, make the killer show his hand. He had hoped for better luck with Diller and the man's disappearance puzzled him. *Was* he the killer? Had Banner scared him off? Unlikely. Five men involved with the hanging of his brother still lived: Harlow, Forester, the sheriff and a deputy, and Sharpe. A man bent on revenge didn't leave the job half-finished. He could only assume some external factor had entered into the equation.

Next came Harlow. He needed an approach to the man. With Franklin and Diller the plan had been to assault dead-on, confront and accuse and see what happened. He doubted that would work with Harlow. The foreman already knew Banner's mission, what he had learned. He had been present during most of the discussions with Forester. And if he played a part in this scheme he had easy access to Banner, would have made some sort of counter move by now — or had he? Had the spook attack been instigated by the foreman? He knew Banner had ridden to October Creek to question Diller. Had he followed? Most of the 'hands had been in town, leaving Harlow pretty much on his own. He said he had gone to town, though Banner hadn't seen him. The saloon was crowded and Banner's attention was elsewhere, so it was possible he had overlooked him.

A long shot, Banner told himself. The foreman had no motive. He worked for the Circle H, why would he rustle from it and the surrounding spreads? He had run across dissatisfied 'hands helping themselves to stock before but Harlow appeared to have little reason to risk that as he stood to inherit his own spread when he married Forester's daughter. It made no sense. And what would he possibly have against the other ranchers?

Banner sighed. Though he couldn't tie Harlow to anything, he took the notion to search the foreman's belongings in the bunkhouse, before determining a course of direct action against the man

That left Silverbird, least likely of the suspects. Silverbird said his stock had diminished, but he might be lying, covering up. Still, by Panhandle standards he had a small spread and it hadn't taken any great bounds in size over the past months. If he were rustling cattle, he had a way of getting rid of them. Like Harlow, he intended to marry Shania, though it would come without Forester's blessing or any part of the Circle H spread as a wedding present. Forester would crush Silverbird's operation in all likelihood. That notion alone might make Silverbird angry enough to want to kill Forester, but what about the other ranchers? Banner couldn't see the gain in it for the youth; he appeared more intent on earning Forester's respect than on stealing cattle and murder. While he couldn't let Silverbird completely off the hook, the youth stayed at the bottom of the list.

Banner led his horse into the livery and loosened the cinch. He stopped in mid-motion, a sound reaching his ears. He listened, unsure what it was or where it had come from at first. Guiding his horse to a stall, he paused to listen again. The sound had been furtive, low, almost a whimper. He felt sure whatever had made it was making a deliberate effort to conceal it now.

Banner walked from the stall and made his way along the aisle. Horses snorted and nickered and the musky aroma of dung and leather and hay assailed his nostrils. Another scent rose above these, pleasant and evocative: perfume. Expensive perfume. His footfalls came light, gliding. In the last stall he found the reason for the noise, and the perfume.

"Ma'am?" He removed his hat and peered at Shania Forester, who lay on a pile of hay. Tears trailed down her face as she looked up. She quickly brushed them away.

"What do you want?" Her voice was sharp, challenging, and she was obviously embarrassed he'd caught her crying. She gained her feet, hurriedly brushing strands of hay from her skirt with an indignant flare.

Banner felt a trifle uncomfortable. "Just returning from town. Heard a noise and wondered what it was."

"Well now you know." She stepped out of the stall.

"You all right?" Genuine concern laced his voice. He had a notion he knew what she was crying about.

She glared at him. "No, I am not all right, Mr Banner. In fact, I am far from it!"

Banner leaned against a stall and removed his hat. "Silverbird?"

Surprise widened her eyes. "How did — ?"

"I met him by the creek the other night, after Harlow dragged you off. We went back to his place and had us a nice talk."

"Then you don't agree with my father?" A note of hope hung in her voice.

"I think you should marry who you want."

Her face brightened and he marvelled at just how beautiful she was.

"Then tell my father that! He wants me to marry Harlow as soon as possible."

"Did, but he told me to mind my own business."

"I love Jim, Mr Banner, and nothing's going to stop me from marrying him, not Harlow and not my father."

Banner frowned. "Jim wants your father's respect. Reckon you oughta give him the chance to earn that."

Her head dropped and she studied something invisible on the floor. Looking up, she gave him a serious look. "I know, but I don't know if I can wait that long. My father might force me to marry Harlow in the meantime."

"Don't see as how he can force you to marry a man you don't love."

She laughed, a bitter sound. "You don't know my father. What can I do, Mr Banner? I'm one woman in a world of cattlemen. They rule everything in these parts and my father rules them. He always has. And he *always* gets his way."

"Don't take me wrong, ma'am, but you strike me as pretty headstrong. Think you can hold your own with your father for a spell and give Silverbird the time he needs. If he can't earn

183

respect by then, you'll have to make your choice."

She gave him a coy look. "I don't know whether to be insulted by that remark or honored by it, Mr Banner."

He gave her a thin smile. "Never would insult a lady."

"You don't strike me as the type to be around many ladies, Mr Banner . . . least not the kind you don't pay for."

He bristled at the remark, but she had read him right so what could he say? "Reckon you're right. A body don't tend to make many ties in my line of work, but I did know a lady once. And I know that if you truly love Silverbird, you'll do whatever it takes to make that love work."

She eyed him, sympathy drifting into her blue eyes. "I get the feeling you've seen chances come and go, Mr Banner."

"Mostly go," he admitted. "Don't let yours pass you by." He turned before she could probe any further into his thoughts. Shania Forester was a perceptive woman, entirely too perceptive, one he could have loved under other circumstances, but love was no longer for him. Not any more.

"Mr Banner . . . " she called after him.

He stopped, turning. "Yes, ma'am?"

"I hope you find what you're looking for. I really do."

He uttered a humorless laugh. "I already found it, Miss Forester. Truly I did."

He put on his hat and walked to the doors, pausing and looking back. She was staring at him and he suddenly wished she and Silverbird would just run away together, live their lives, before something — or someone — interfered.

"Where's Harlow?" he asked, feeling a sudden need to occupy his mind with other thoughts.

She gave him a curious look. "Out on the spread somewhere, I imagine.

Usually is, doing whatever the hell it is he does at this time."

"You don't have much respect for him, do you?"

"Oh, I suppose he's all right, at least he would be — long as he marries someone else." She giggled, a bit more of her self-confidence in the expression.

He left, wondering if fate would prove kinder to Shania Forester and Jim Silverbird than it had to Luke Banner.

* * *

He scanned the vicinity of the bunkhouse for any sign of Harlow or the 'hands before going in. Easing the door shut behind him, he surveyed the rows of beds and sparse furnishings — a few tables, trunks, hard-back chairs. The heavy odor of sweat, dung and Durham hung in the air. Most of the beds were unmade. A long table stood off to the side where the 'hands probably held impromptu poker games for lesser stakes than the ones in town, or when the doves relieved them of their thirty-a-month.

The bunkhouse presented him with a slight dilemma. He had no idea which bunk belonged to Harlow. That meant searching all of them. He began his search by patting down mattresses. A few bunks sported trunks to their sides or beneath; these required more time. None held anything of value except to its owner — tintypes of loved ones, small trinkets given by past girlfriends, boiled shirts or meetin' clothes. Certainly nothing to indicate involvement in the spook killings.

Reaching the halfway mark, he discovered a chest at the side of one of the bunks that gave him pause. More ornate than the others, somewhat larger, it likely belonged to the foreman. He knelt and lifted the lid. It was packed with clothes, papers, though no pictures or anything of a particularly personal nature, as if the foreman came from nowhere, had no ties. That was nothing unusual in itself: plenty of cowhands were drifters, men, for all intents and purposes, without pasts and with probably little future. Men who drifted from spread to spread across the West, sometimes disappearing into the horizon never to be seen again. Harlow, a hard man, looked the type, though if he married Forester's daughter his future would be assured.

The click of a hammer being drawn back snapped his reverie.

With an icy trickle of dread down his spine, Luke Banner knew for the second time in as many days he had been caught unawares. Intent on the job at hand, he had neglected what was going on behind him. He cursed himself, easing the lid shut and turning his head.

Dustin Harlow stood just inside the door, levering a gun at Banner's back. "That could rightly be considered an invasion of privacy, Mr Banner. I could kill you for that."

Banner eyed the man, judging whether the threat was serious. There was something in Harlow's eyes, but what? Banner decided it wasn't murder at this point.

Banner held his voice steady. "That would cause you a little trouble, seein' as how your boss hired me."

"Didn't hire you to go through the men's personals."

"This yours?" He nodded to the chest.

"Reckon that ain't none of your goddamn business."

"You can put the gun away." Banner stood, reasonably sure Harlow wasn't trigger happy. The foreman's hand was perfectly steady and a killing here would be tough to explain to Forester. He didn't think Harlow branding himself a killer would do anything for his chances of marrying Shania, either.

Harlow hesitated then slid the gun into the holster at his hip.

"You don't like me much, do you,

Banner?" Harlow took a step towards him.

"Don't have a reason to, Harlow. Don't have a reason to dislike you, neither." A lie and Harlow picked right up on it.

"But you do anyway. I can see it in your eyes."

Banner shrugged. "Don't matter none. Won't get in the way of my job."

"You don't belong messin' in things, Banner."

A vague sense of memory stirred in his mind, but it remained elusive, fleeting. "What do you mean?"

Harlow took another step towards him.

"Heard from Forester you said Shania shouldn't marry me." The foreman had something in his craw; Banner knew the look well, the look of a man about to step on a rattler.

He made an attempt at diffusing the situation. "Didn't say that. Told him she should make up her own mind.

Told her the same thing."

Harlow's face reddened. "Ain't none of your business, manhunter. You best stick to your job."

"Maybe it ain't my business, but I got a feeling you don't aim to let her make her own choice."

"Why should I? Forester wants her to marry me; that's all that counts. I got our future all laid out and it don't involve her marryin' no half-breed."

Banner saw it was coming. And saw no way to avoid it. Saw it and met it head-on.

Harlow lunged, looping a fist at Banner's head.

Banner ducked, snapping a right that buried itself in Harlow's breadbasket. Harlow let out an *oomph* and staggered. Banner rushed him, but the foreman was strong, quick to recover.

Harlow arced a fist that ricocheted from Banner's jaw. A spray of stars exploded before his eyes. A second blow followed and Banner stumbled backwards, going over a bunk and slamming into the floor.

He swiped blood away from his lips and groped for his senses, shaking his head to clear his vision.

Harlow sprang over the bunk and landed on top of him. They rolled, Harlow doing his damnedest to brain the manhunter with a hammering fist and Banner doing his damnedest to avoid it.

Jamming both hands against Harlow's chest, he arched his back and thrust with all his strength. Harlow flew back and Banner gained his feet. He delivered a chopping punch that took Harlow in the chest as he came to his knees.

The blow stopped Harlow in his tracks, but only for an instant. The foreman recovered with surprising speed and vaulted to his feet. He launched another looping blow, which Banner easily countered. The manhunter sent a left into the foreman's jaw.

The burly ranch worker took a double-step backwards and Banner charged him. Harlow grunted, let go a haymaker Banner couldn't completely avoid. The blow was glancing but powerful. It stunned him. Harlow's punches landed like horse kicks. He prayed the man's stamina didn't match his strength.

Summoning all he had left, Banner rushed Harlow again, colliding, sending them both backwards into the wall. Harlow's back slammed into it hard and his head bounced from the board. Air exploded from his lungs. A dazed look crossed his eyes.

Banner manoeuvred into position for another blow, one that would end the battle, but the man wasn't as stunned as he thought.

The foreman jerked up a knee and Banner twisted, but not enough. The blow took him on the side of the leg and he staggered back, Harlow in immediate pursuit.

Harlow hit him again and Banner went down, head reeling, jaw throbbing.

The foreman lunged and Banner, out

of pure reflex, brought his legs up. His boots thudded into the foreman's chest, hurling him backwards.

Gasping, Banner felt nausea twist in his belly. He forced himself to his feet, just as Harlow came at him again. Christamighty, the man had the tenacity of a bull in the rutting season. Banner sidestepped, throwing a chopping heel-hand to the foreman's temple. Harlow took a stuttering step and sprawled face-down across the bunk. Banner whirled, lunging.

He pounced on top of the stunned foreman and grabbed a handful of hair, jerking up Harlow's head.

"That's enough!" he said through gritted teeth, gasping. "It's over."

"The hell it is!" the foreman spat back, blood flecking the corners of his mouth. "We'll go 'round again and next time I won't take any chances."

Banner let him go and backed to the door. Harlow leaned against the bed, wiping blood from his lips and glaring.

"Neither will I, Harlow. You can rest assured of that."

Harlow uttered a hoarse laugh. "You stay away from Shania, you hear? You do the job you was hired for and no more."

Banner left the bunkhouse on unsteady legs, feeling more pain in his body than he had in ages.

9

THE next day Luke Banner felt as though mules had stomped across his face and good many parts of his body.

You're gettin' old. A few years ago you would have cleaned his clock.

Taking a deep breath and wincing, he discovered none of his ribs were cracked. He flexed his fingers and rolled his shoulders. His head felt like a stick of dynamite had exploded inside it.

Banner climbed from bed and went to the bureau where he splashed water from a porcelain basin into his face. Toweling off, he found a boiled shirt the servants had prepared for him and dressed. Strapping on his gun belt, he went downstairs. Starving, he downed a breakfast of bacon and eggs and sourdough biscuits in record time, then washed it down with three cups of strong Arbuckle's.

The brawl with Harlow stuck in his craw but curiosity about what might be in the foreman's trunk overshadowed that. He wondered if Harlow had instigated the confrontation to prevent him from searching further. Or had it merely been for the reason the man had stated, to keep him from meddling in his affairs where Shania Forester was concerned? Was the man hiding something? Was he simply territorial? Whatever the case, Banner wanted another look at that trunk, but he had to be more careful next time. Excuse notwithstanding, Banner had seen cold fury in the foreman's eyes. Hatred? Maybe. One thing was definite: he had relished the opportunity to strike.

Banner wandered outside, gazing across the spread. The sun was peeking above the horizon in a blaze of orange and gold and the sky was clear and rosy. The smoky scents of bacon and Durham drifted from the bunkhouse.

He saw hands preparing for the day, saddling horses, tending to chores. A second search had to wait, possibly even a few days. Harlow would surely be on his guard.

Banner considered his next step, deciding he still had too many unanswered questions about Franklin and Harlow. Looking for an answer meant risking the sheriff's wrath, but he saw no choice. He had set his bait with all suspects except Silverbird and only two ranchers remained. The spook would make its next move soon, so Banner couldn't afford to delay.

He still needed a motive. And that's what he'd set out to nail down today.

He sauntered into the livery and saddled his bay. Mounting, he peered out at the spread and for the briefest of moments, he recollected Jamie again, the life he was never to have. A deep melancholy arose within him, but he shook it off, gigging his horse into motion and riding in the direction of October Creek.

The streets of October Creek were just starting to come alive. The sun had notched higher in the sky, coating the settlement with a golden sheen that belied the tarnish beneath.

He glanced at the sheriff's office and rode on until he reached the telegram shack at the opposite end of town. The telegraph clerk looked up from beneath a visor and yawned as Banner entered.

"Mornin'," the operator grumbled. Banner tipped his hat. He took a slip of paper and scribbled a message, a request for information from a friend, care of the Pinkerton Agency. He needed a check on all his suspects: Franklin, Harlow, Silverbird, Diller, even Forester and Sharpe, the remaining rancher. He hoped it might provide his motive.

He paid the operator and stayed to watch him tap out the message.

Taking his time riding back to the Circle H, he let thoughts turn over in his mind. While he hoped his query would narrow the field, he couldn't depend on it. His focus shifted to the remaining ranchers, Forester and Sharpe. Who would be the spook's next victim? Forester appeared the better protected. Sharpe? Seemed likely. But if Banner watched Sharpe, that left Forester vulnerable. Sharpe likely had men posted, least if he had a lick of sense. That might make things more difficult for the killer.

As he reached the outskirts of the Circle H, he noticed a handful of longhorns bunched and grazing to his left. The beasts were huge, with thick slabs of muscle and razor-tipped curved horns that could span six feet. One of the animals cast him a weary eye and he let a thin smile touch his lips.

"Easy fella, ain't me you got to worry about." He edged his bay closer as he passed the steers. Something caught his eye. Drawing up, his brow crinkled. The brands. Two different ones and neither belonged to Forester. The first he recognized instantly, a Double L.

That belonged to Hadley, the murdered rancher. The other, a Slash L, if he remembered correctly, was owned by Stiller. What were Stiller and Hadley's animals doing on Circle H property? He contemplated it a moment, then heeled his horse into an easy, ground-eating gait. Mismatched steers on Circle H land. A suspicion rose in his mind, possibly a motive for the killings. He smiled, knowing he had only to confirm it.

Hitching his horse in front of the main house, he went in and located Caleb Forester in the kitchen, just finishing up his breakfast.

Forester turned to him, nodding. "You're up with the roosters this morning, aren't you?"

"Had an errand in town to attend to."

"That's a little risky, ain't it? Best not let Franklin get wind of it."

"Last I knew, he didn't set my itinerary." Banner walked over and poured himself a cup of coffee.

"What happened to you?" asked Forester, glancing at the bruises and scuffs on the manhunter's face.

"You might say Harlow and I had ourselves a difference of opinion. He didn't tell you?"

Forester shook his head. "Neglected to mention it. What about?"

"He figures I should keep my opinions about your daughter to myself."

"Harlow's a good man, if a bit territorial — but I admire that in a man. You'd best take his advice."

Banner ignored the remark. He had other things on his mind. "On my way in I noticed some steers that carried Stiller and Hadley's brands on their flanks." He broached it matter-of-factly, inviting Forester to take the lead.

The rancher nodded, setting a cup on the counter and pouring himself a coffee. "What of it?"

"Wondered why, is all."

Forester shrugged. "The Association kept a tight agreement: we'd work

202

together but if one rancher was killed accidentally the others would divvy up the stock."

"Killed accidentally, or murdered?"

"Or murdered. Sharpe and I have increased our stock ten-thousand head each."

Forester's statement confirmed Banner's suspicions. "That means bigger profits."

"I won't be complainin', neither will Sharpe."

"If you live that long."

Forester's face turned grim. "What's that s'posed to mean?"

Banner took a chair and leaned back, taking a sip of coffee before answering. "Just that whoever's left stands to be sittin' pretty; no amount of rustlin' could compare to that, give that much power and profit."

Forester's brow furrowed. "Hear, Banner, what are you sayin'? Are you accusing — "

"Ain't accusin' no one, Forester. But you gotta admit whoever's left standing, you or Sharpe, reckons to be the biggest cattleman this side of Chisum."

Forester's expression softened. "I see what you mean. Then Sharpe could — "

"Sharpe or *you*."

"That's preposterous! I hired you to stop the murders!"

"I'm inclined to agree with you there. 'Course you could be just makin' an attempt to cover things up, but that's a dangerous game when you hire someone like me."

"What are you sayin', Banner? Am I guilty or not?"

"Don't think you are."

"Then it *is* Sharpe."

Banner shook his head. "Maybe not him, either. Might be someone else entirely."

Forester appeared puzzled. "Who?"

"Ain't prepared to say just yet. I sent some telegrams today that might help me figure that out. If not, we'll have to take some chances bangin' woodpiles."

"Chase the real killer out, you mean?"

"Exactly."

"And in the meantime?"

Banner stood. "In the meantime I think we pay Sharpe a visit and see what he thinks. Maybe it'll give us some fresh insight."

"I'll saddle up," said Forester.

★ ★ ★

Clayton Sharpe would be of no help to anyone. Banner knew that as soon as they came within range of the rancher's house. A throng of men had gathered outside the dwelling, each showing a look of concern or worry. An ominous murmur went through the band and Banner knew what they would find when they entered the house: the field had been narrowed to one; the spook had struck again.

Banner and Forester drew up and tethered their horses. Forester stepped up to the nearest man and asked,

"What in tarnation happened?"

"Sharpe got his neck stretched sometime durin' the night," the man said, eyes darting. "They got that half-breed in there all trussed up. Looks like he's the galldamn spook!"

Banner tensed at the announcement and Forester grunted, looking back at him.

"Looks like you'll be out of a job, Banner. Told you there ain't no good Injuns." Forester brushed past the man and went into the house, Banner following.

Inside the sheriff and deputy stood in the parlor where Clayton Sharpe still dangled from a rope slung over a beam in the ceiling. Banner gave the boy the once-over then eyed the sheriff, who looked at him with an expression of undisguised animosity.

"Why haven't you cut him down?" Banner noted by the color and bloat of the features Sharpe had been hanging a few hours.

Franklin shrugged, making a face.

"He's dead; don't make no never-mind to him."

Banner grunted with disgust and went to the body, unsheathing his bowie knife and slicing through the rope. He lowered the dead rancher gently to the floor.

"Show some goddamn respect," said Forester to the sheriff, who merely offered a smug expression.

Banner's gaze shifted to the young man sitting on the floor near the wall. Jim Silverbird sat rubbing the back of his head and looking dazed.

Forester eyed the youth and uttered a low laugh. "You got yourself in a heap of trouble, boy. Don't guess you'll be doin' any marryin' anytime soon."

The sheriff laughed. "Found him right with the body. Looks like we got ourselves a killer."

Banner let out a grunt of derision. "That boy's no more a killer than Forester."

"That so, Mr Banner? And how might you come by that notion? Caught him dead to rights. He was lyin' right on the floor next to the corpse."

"You think it's likely he'd hang Sharpe then stick around to wait for the law? Where's his spook costume?"

"Reckon he wanted to throw suspicion off himself. With all the ranchers dead there'd be no one else to blame and we'd naturally suspect him. Sharpe had men posted; they saw him ride in and didn't figure anything was wrong. The didn't see no one else, spook included."

Banner scoffed. "That's ludicrous! Looks to me like he was just in the wrong place at the wrong time." The manhunter turned to Silverbird, who looked up with a stunned expression. "Why don't you tell 'em that, son?"

The 'breed started to speak but Forester cut him off. "Can't you see what's in front of your face, Banner? The boy's a no-good. Probably figured by killin' off everyone else he could rustle steers."

Banner shook his head. "Makes no

sense. He don't have the operation to handle rustlin'. 'Sides, you could put him out of business anytime you wanted."

Forester snorted. "Looks like I should have 'fore now. That's what I get for being soft-hearted."

"I didn't do it, Mr Forester," Jim Silverbird spoke up. "I only came here to talk to Sharpe and try to help. Someone hit me from behind."

"Tell that to the hangin' judge, boy," said Franklin, fingering his badge.

"Who's that?" asked Banner, knowing the answer.

"Me." Franklin's tone was cold, yet strangely cheerful.

Banner walked over to Silverbird and knelt, hand going to the back of the boy's head. The youth flinched and the manhunter turned, looking at Forester.

"He's got a lump the size of a rooster's egg on the back of his head. I think he's tellin' the truth."

Forester shook his head. "Reckon he

put that there himself to make it look good." Banner saw a hint of doubt in the rancher's eyes. He quickly hid it and walked out.

Banner stood alone with the sheriff, deputy and Silverbird. Going to the youth, the deputy pulled him to his feet and lashed his hands behind his back.

"You'll hang at sunrise, boy," said Franklin and Banner felt a spike of unease pierce his belly. He felt convinced the youth was telling the truth, though he had made a damn fool move coming here to talk to Sharpe. He had likely stumbled on to the spook about to murder the rancher and the real killer had snatched at a perfect opportunity to frame the boy for the killings. But how could Banner prove something like that in time to save the 'breed's life? The sheriff wouldn't believe a word of it and likely wouldn't accept evidence to the contrary: he had his scapegoat, his easy answer, the way he had with Bob Diller. Banner studied Franklin, seeing conviction in his eyes.

He wanted this boy accused and hanged for a reason and Banner had a damn good idea what that might be.

The deputy guided Silverbird from the room and the youth gave Banner a pleading look as he passed, a request for help from the only possible source.

"Tell Shania I love her, Mr Banner. Please do that for me." His voice was steady but edged with worry.

The manhunter nodded. The deputy took him out and Banner heard the jeers of the 'hands. Bloodlust in their voices, they shouted for a hanging. Franklin would give it to them all too gleefully.

Banner rode back to the Circle H, mulling over the situation with no great confidence in his ability to exonerate the youth. Silverbird would hang at dawn and that would be the end of it. Or would it? Forester would be left alive. He would virtually rule the Panhandle, adding Sharpe's considerable stock to his own, as well as Silverbird's measly head count. Forester would be a giant of the West, a name set down in history books right besides the likes of Chisum and the other cattle barons.

Or would he?

The reason behind this was still unclear and unresolved. Forester wasn't the one killing off ranchers in an effort to build himself an empire; that much Banner felt sure of. He was already rich and though he conceivably wanted to be richer, he wouldn't have bothered forming the Forester Cattlemen's Association had his plan been to eliminate the competition. Whoever was behind the scheme had more in mind than just blaming Silverbird and letting it lie. In all likelihood, Forester would meet with an untimely end and Banner bet it wouldn't take long, though he figured the spook thing would be abandoned hereafter. Whoever was responsible would take pains to make it look like an accident.

His thoughts went back to Silverbird.

He wasn't the killer, either. That point had been made all too clear by finding him at the scene of the murder. He was merely unlucky enough to stumble into the situation, that was all. He might well die for his error in judgement, but he would be another innocent victim.

Banner made up his mind to help the boy, even if it meant bucking Franklin. In fact, he found himself relishing the possibility. One way or another — by clearing the boy's name or breaking him out of prison — Banner would see to it Silverbird didn't hang.

At the moment, however, he reckoned he had another problem. With the 'breed in jail for the killings, he was out of a job. He expected Forester would inform him of as much when he reached the Circle H. That made finding the true killer all the more difficult. But when Banner hired on to the case, he'd neglected to inform Forester of one thing: regardless of pay, once he took a case, he saw it through to his *own* satisfaction, no one else's. Nothing short of a bullet would stop him.

He drew up in front of the main house. He noticed the door open and Forester's horse tied to the rail. As he crossed the veranda, the sound of the rancher's angry voice rang from inside. He located him, along with Shania and Harlow, in the parlor. The young woman was slumped in a chair, tears streaming from her eyes. Forester's face was red and tense and Harlow's eyes carried a peculiar gleam of satisfaction. The foreman gazed at Banner with a look of contempt then tried to lend a comforting hand to Shania, who brushed him away.

Forester's attention shifted to Banner briefly, then back to his daughter. "I'm sorry I have to tell you this, Shania, but you got to know. He's a killer, plain and simple. I couldn't let you throw your life away."

"Go to hell!" she screeched. "He isn't a killer and you know it!"

Harlow opened his mouth to say

something but Forester waved him off. "We caught him dead to rights. He was with Sharpe's body."

She gave him a cutting look. "That proves nothing! What reason would he have to kill Sharpe, or any of the others for that matter? There has to be some explanation." Her lips set in a tight line and her tearful gaze slipped to Banner, as if asking his help. Forester shot the manhunter a look that told him to keep quiet; he had no desire to have his daughter filled with the foolish notion Silverbird had been set up.

The rancher's attention turned back to his daughter. "Reckon he wanted to take their stock for his own, rustle it off whoever's spread was left."

Shania vaulted to her feet, and she went to the window, folding her arms and staring out. "That's ridiculous, Father. Jim was makin' his own way. He's as honest as they come, too honest in fact. All he wanted was your respect. I knew you had your petty little hates, but I never thought it would get in the way of your sense of fairness and justice."

A great debate seemed to rage behind the rancher's eyes as he stared at his daughter. He sighed a heavy sigh and took a step towards her. "Injuns killed your uncle, Shania. I didn't want to tell you that, but you give me no choice. That's why I hate 'em. They're used to killin'; it's the way they live."

She whirled, anger blazing in her eyes, face set with fury. "No, it isn't their way of life. They wanted to protect what was theirs. We did the same to them, maybe worse. Jim is no killer, no matter what you say, and if he goes, I go with him!"

Forester's face tightened. "You know I don't cotton to that kind of forward talk. They're all savages in my book. Silverbird ain't goin' nowhere and you ain't goin', neither."

"What do you mean by that?" Her lower lip started to quiver as realization dawned in her eyes. She knew what her father was about to say.

"Silverbird'll hang for murder at dawn, no way around it. And you'll marry Harlow within a week. You have no choice."

"No!" she blurted, hands going to her mouth. "I won't let them hang him!"

"No way to stop it, Shania. Best to accept the truth and face it."

Harlow took a step towards her, as if intending to comfort her but she gave him a glare that stopped him dead in his tracks. "I won't marry you, you sonofabitch! No matter what happens, I won't!" She dashed off, rushing up the stairs. Banner heard a door slam. He looked at Harlow.

Harlow grinned. "Reckon we won't be needin' your services no longer, manhunter." The foreman took great pleasure in saying it and Banner felt like shooting him on the spot. He restrained himself, though it took some effort.

"Go tend to your duties," Forester suddenly ordered, motioning for Harlow to leave. Banner felt more than a little surprised and Harlow appeared shocked. He glared at Banner and brushed past him hard, departing the house.

When the manhunter turned back to the rancher, Forester was looking at him sharply.

"Despite what you may think of me, Banner, I love my daughter and her happiness is what's most important to me. I hate Injuns, hate them with all my soul, but . . ."

Banner finished it for him. "You don't want to take the chance another innocent man will be hanged." The look that passed between them was chilled but telling. Banner had hit upon Forester's thought exactly.

"I'll pay you an extra day. I won't have Shania accusing me of being unfair when this is all over. You find strong evidence tellin' me the boy ain't guilty and I'll consider it."

"You'll stop the hanging?"

Forester sighed, "I ain't makin'

promises. I'd just as soon see a dead Injun as a live one, but I been doin' some thinkin' and I reckon I got enough of one ghost to live with. I don't need another."

Banner nodded. "You know he ain't guilty, don't you?"

"I know nothing of the sort, Mr Banner, but if I don't show the effort Shania will never forgive me. That's somethin' I ain't prepared to live with."

Forester's eyes said otherwise, but Banner let it go. For the moment he had a reprieve, though damn little time to work with. The youth would hang at sun-up and the killer would likely lie low until it was over. The spook would vanish into the western night forever.

10

THE day was passing faster than Luke Banner would have liked. The late-afternoon sun blazed in the lower quarter of the sky, edging towards the western horizon.

He had little time left in which to save Jim Silverbird's neck.

While surprised at Forester's decision to retain his services, Banner found it had provided him little advantage in clearing Silverbird's name. He had gone to the 'breed's homestead and searched, discovering nothing, then headed back to Sharpe's ranch to try his luck there. A ranchhand challenged him, though not seriously, giving him run of the place after he explained why he was there. He had acted on Forester's authority and the 'hand had acquiesced.

A survey of the dead rancher's place yielded no clues and a thorough questioning of the workers turned up nothing — all corroborated the sheriff's decree: the 'breed had ridden in and killed Sharpe. None had seen him do the deed, but many had seen him enter. No one else. Still, it was dark and the spook, wearing black, might easily have snuck in. Banner placed the killer inside when Silverbird had shown up; that's the way it had to be for him to get the jump on the youth. He had blundered in unsuspecting and been pistol-whipped.

The lack of progress frustrated Banner. His nerves felt cinched, raw with anxiousness, as he guided his bay along one of the corrals. Scattered things had begun to piece together in his mind, but there were still missing parts. He had one last chance; the telegram. He'd ride to town in a short piece to collect his answer and hoped that would clear up some of the mystery. He suspected a motive, but needed proof to confront the killer, flush him out. If that didn't pan out . . .

Well, then he would try what every good poker player became a master of: the bluff. It was his only option.

The motive. Banner felt sure it involved the acquisition of steers from the ranches. When one rancher met death, his stock passed to the rest. With all ranchers dead, Forester gained all, even Silverbird's after the boy got his necktie party. However, Banner felt convinced Caleb Forester would never live to enjoy the benefits of the monopoly. Someone else would, and that someone had orchestrated a carefully laid plan that would reach fruition if Banner didn't stop it.

Banner's view of the surly rancher had softened a bit since their last talk. The rancher *was* genuinely more concerned about his daughter than his own welfare, he had to be to put aside his prejudice and give Banner free reign to clear Silverbird. If Jim Silverbird hanged, Shania Forester would hate her father. The old man knew that and that had heavily influenced his decision, but there was more to it. Caleb Forester had an innocent's man's blood on his hands and he would never be able to wash them clean. He was not about to have another's.

A yell tore Banner from his thoughts. He looked up to see Hinkley riding hell-bent for the main house. Banner swung into the saddle and gigged his horse into a gallop in an effort to intercept him before he reached the building. He angled his bay around in front of the hand, cutting him off.

The man slowed, face red. "Banner!" He gasped, placing a hand on his chest and struggling for breath.

"Hold up, son," Banner kept his voice calm, reassuring, though his own heart pounded and his curiosity was aroused. "What's on your mind?"

The 'hand eyed him, sucking long breaths. "Was down by the arroyo, herdin' some steers that had wandered a bit back towards the open grazeland. Saw, saw somethin' tangled in the brush by the side of the stream."

Banner's heart skipped a beat. "What was it, son?"

"A body, by Christ, I swear it was! Didn't git close enough to have me a look-see, but I could tell by the way it was tangled and lyin' it was a body."

Banner's belly tightened. "Whose?"

"Dunno. Like I said, wasn't about to get any closer. Don't get paid enough for that. Was headin' back to tell Mr Forester 'bout it so he could fetch the sheriff."

Banner nodded. "Tell Forester, and tell him I'll handle it and get the sheriff myself."

The 'hand appeared to think it over. "Your call, Mr Banner. Forester hired you to take care of such."

Banner scooted his horse sideways and the hand arrowed for the main house. Banner gigged his horse into motion, heading for the arroyo. He knew who that body belonged to, and if he were right one of his suspects was permanently removed from the list.

★ ★ ★

Banner slowed as he approached the arroyo. A bubbling stream, which fed the creek, meandered through the fissure. Stone walls rose fifty feet up to either side. The ground sloped, became rocky, treacherous, so he drew up and dismounted, going ahead on foot. The 'hand hadn't given him specific directions, but Banner had a good notion where the body would be. The 'hand said he'd been guiding cattle back on to grazeland and Banner caught sight of them bunched off to his left. The body would be within sighting distance of them.

He spotted the corpse immediately. Making his way to the stream bank, he saw the form lying face down, tangled in heavy brush. As he drew closer, he noticed it was fairly intact, which meant it had been placed there recently because the buzzards hadn't gone to work on it.

Kneeling, he gripped a stiffened

shoulder and turned the body over. He was right: the corpse was fresh; the stiffness had just set in and there was still a smattering of warmth. A bloodless hole showed in the victim's forehead. One bullet had done the trick, fired at close range.

It wasn't a pretty sight, but it told Banner all he needed to know. A quiet rage boiled within him as his gaze lifted to the distance. The sun was going down on the Panhandle and within the hour it would go down on a killer, a blood-thirsty devil who would atone for all crimes past and present, leaving only a murderer in the guise of a spook to deal with.

★ ★ ★

Banner drew up in front of Sheriff Franklin's office. He had all he needed, now. First making a stop at the telegraph office and retrieving his replies, he found his friend at the Pinkerton Agency had come through.

226

Two suspects had panned out. Although he got mostly what he expected, one fact mildly surprised him and that he would let Forester know about when he returned to the ranch. Meanwhile Sheriff Franklin was going to answer for a number of indiscretions past and present, and by the time Banner finished, Jim Silverbird would be a free man.

He dismounted and gazed at the sheriff's door.

The sun dipped behind the horizon and weird shadows stretched across the street. Uttering a thin laugh, he moved across the boardwalk with icy surety and grim confidence.

Franklin, who sat at his desk cleaning a gun, looked up and slapped the piece shut as Banner stepped in. He tensed, noting the hard look welded to the manhunter's face. He eased his hand away from the gun, knowing it would be suicide to try anything while facing Banner.

"What the hell do you want?"

Franklin's tone rang challenging and false, designed to hide his fear, and Banner gave him a thin smile. He walked to the desk and tossed down the telegrams.

Franklin eyed them, Banner, the telegrams again. He slowly reached out and picked them up, reading each.

"So? Don't really tell you nothin' 'bout me you didn't already know or suspect."

Banner nodded. "True enough. A bit more, I reckon, but I've seen your type often enough to know the score."

Franklin averted Banner's stare. "Don't amount to beans, even the other."

"Inclined to disagree with you on that. You're involved with something no lawman should be." Banner glanced over at the row of cells. Jim Silverbird sat on the edge of a cot, peering at him with a look of hope.

"You got no proof. I got my killer right there in that cell. He'll hang at dawn and that will end it. These don't mean a thing." He flung the telegrams on the desk.

Banner came directly to the point. "I want you to release Silverbird. Now."

Franklin brayed a laugh. "You lost your galldamn mind? Kid's guilty of murder, Banner. Can't rightly see lettin' him free."

"*You're* guilty of murder, Franklin. I know that, now."

Franklin's eyes narrowed and deep creases lined his forehead. A thin coating of sweat broke out on his brow. "Like I said, you got no proof and it ain't too all-fired likely you could make anything stick on me."

"I bet I can make it stick on your partner; my guess is he'll sing like a bird to anybody who'll listen if I make him a deal not to stretch his neck." Franklin looked suddenly uncomfortable. The statement held only a glimmer of truth. The manhunter had no intention of cutting deals with anyone. The guilty man would hang, or die by the gun. That much was fact in Banner's mind.

Franklin looked at Silverbird, who had risen and come to the bars. He looked back to Banner, who held his gaze. "You're bluffin'." He said it with little confidence.

"Am I? Before I came here I was out by the arroyo."

Franklin's face went white.

"Found me a body, a fresh one. You put it there."

Franklin blinked, fear a rattlesnake in his eyes. "Don't know what you're talkin' about, Banner. I ain't got nothin' to do with this."

"You're responsible for that body, though at first I wondered why it was fresh. Reckon I got the answer to that. Has something to do with Jim, doesn't it?"

Franklin's eyes glazed with a desperate look.

Banner smiled inwardly, gaze shifting about the room, settling on a ring of keys dangling from a nail. He went to them, lifted them off. "I'm taking the boy with me. He's innocent and after tonight everyone will know it." Banner gripped the keys with his left hand. He presented his back at an angle that allowed him to watch Franklin from the corner of his eyes. He saw the sheriff's gaze dart to his gun. That was what Banner hoped for.

He wasn't disappointed.

Franklin's hand flashed towards the piece. Desperation overriding fear, he intended to shoot Banner in the back. He was cornered and by dawn he would be swinging from a noose. Banner had given him no choice.

Franklin snatched up the gun, lifted it, brought it almost level.

Banner's right hand slapped to his Peacemaker. The piece cleared leather as he whirled.

A shot thundered, deafening, final. The gun dropped from Franklin's grip and a shock exploded on his avuncular face. A crimson blotch ripened on his belly. He looked down, seeing his life's blood gush out, both hands gripping the hole and trying to staunch the flow. Scarlet streamed between his fingers. His mouth opened and he fell backwards like an axed tree, crashing to the floor.

The manhunter holstered his Peacemaker and turned to Silverbird, whose face held a sickened expression.

"No other way, son," Banner assured him, as he went to the cell door and unlocked it. "He was dead set on hangin' you for the murders and he was a killer."

Jim Silverbird nodded, swallowing hard. "He killed the ranchers?"

Banner shook his head. "No, reckon not. But he helped in this whole thing and he damn sure killed the fella at the arroyo."

"Then who — "

"I'll tell you that on the way back to the Circle H."

★ ★ ★

Banner and Silverbird rode hard for the Circle H. The manhunter explained the facts to the 'breed on the first leg of the trip, that Sheriff Franklin had gotten what he deserved — justice — for his part in the crimes, but he wasn't the actual mastermind of the spook scheme. That honor belonged to another, who had merely to complete his plan by killing Forester and marrying the rancher's daughter. Silverbird's face waxed serious and for the briefest of instances, Banner considered leaving the youth behind. He knew the look, the sudden slow fire that burned behind the 'breed's gaze. Jim Silverbird saw someone he loved threatened; he would do anything to protect her. That could lead to a mistake Banner could little afford. The boy was eager, too eager, to prove himself to Forester and that coupled with simmering rage, meant trouble. The decision was difficult: he had little right to stop the 'breed, especially in light of what he had experienced in his own life.

After careful thought he decided on letting the boy come. In truth, he wasn't sure he could have stopped him. The boy needed his chance and who was he to rob him of that? Any scars could be borne later.

They reached the outskirts of the Circle H. Night had fallen and moonlight frosted the Plains. In the distance, lights blazed from the compound buildings. The stillness was eerie, befitting: the spook had appeared from the moon-glazed blackness and tonight Banner would see to it that's where he would return.

The manhunter slowed, angling towards the bunkhouse. Would the killer be there? Try to stop him? That would be best. An isolated place with no risk to Forester or his daughter. And this time he wouldn't be caught unawares.

He drew up before the building, Silverbird coming to a stop beside him. Dismounting, a look passed between them. Silverbird drew his gun, which he'd retrieved from a drawer in the sheriff's desk, but Banner placed a hand over it, forcing him to reholster.

"Let me handle that, son. No need for you to make yourself a killer in her eyes."

Silverbird started to object, but apparently decided Banner was right. "What do you want here?"

"The killer. If not, proof to bring to Forester." He took the steps in a single leap and shoved the door open. Two men half-rose from their bunks, stopping when they saw the look in his eyes. He reckoned the majority of the men were on their way to the saloon; they'd passed a number of them on their way in.

He felt somewhat disappointed the foreman wasn't here because that meant he was at the main house. Banner didn't like it. The risk had jumped a few notches. He went to the foreman's trunk and lifted the lid.

"Whatta you aim to find, Mr Banner?" Silverbird asked, a curious look in his eyes.

"A spook." He rummaged through

clothes and belongings, tossing them onto the bed until he found a large strongbox. Heaving it onto the bunk, he studied the sturdy lock attached.

"Looks like he didn't want nobody gettin' into it," Silverbird said, eyeing the lock.

"Surprised he didn't move it. Musta figured the lock was good enough and nobody'd suspect him anyway." Banner stood. "Stand clear." He drew his gun and fired. The lock shattered and the top popped open. Reholstering, he lifted the lid, peering at the contents.

"Judas Priest!" said Silverbird.

The manhunter lifted out a folded black duster, black trousers and shirt, battered Stetson. Beneath the garments was a compartment, which he opened. It contained a white paste of some sort, a number of rubbery appliances and a bottle containing a brownish substance.

"What the hell is it?" Silverbird asked, puzzled.

Banner touched the paste and spread

a bit of it across the back of his hand. "Theatrical makeup. The rest are rubber appliances actors use to build up their faces. They stick it on with the gum in that bottle. In the dark it'd be damn hard to believe you weren't seein' a spook."

"You knew the spook wasn't real?"

"Yep. Hit him when he cornered me at Diller's place. A little came off on my hand and it was obvious there wasn't no real goblin hauntin' the Panhandle."

Silverbird nodded. Banner grabbed the hat and duster and carried them to the door. Turning, he eyed the 'hands, who stared with a mixture of fear and confusion. "There's your spook, men. Reckon his hauntin' days are about over."

The manhunter went outside and mounted, heeling his horse towards the main house, Silverbird following suit.

Light blazed from the structure, throwing a buttery glow across the veranda. Banner and Silverbird reined up and tethered their horses.

Banner looked at the youth. "If he's in there, son, don't make any moves on him, you understand? I got a notion he's gonna act like a cornered coyote and I don't want nobody gettin' hurt who don't deserve to."

Silverbird nodded, but Banner knew the boy would do anything to protect Shania and that meant he couldn't be completely trusted.

They moved across the veranda and eased open the door. Banner felt ice settle in his belly. Harlow stood in the parlor with Shania and Caleb Forester. The young woman's face was pinched, features pale and drawn. She had been crying if the puffiness under her blue eyes was any indication. Banner imagined Forester had been working on her again to marry Harlow. Her face brightened when she saw Banner come in with Silverbird, but the foreman gave them a glare of hate and fury. Banner stepped into the room, tossing the garments on to the settee.

"Reckon these belong to you, Harlow." His tone came cold, deliberate. Harlow made an effort not to look at the garments, but his face betrayed momentary shock.

"What the hell are you talkin' about, Banner?" demanded Forester indignantly. His posture stiffened and he nudged his head towards the outfit. "What are those? And why the devil did you bring that Injun to my house?" Hate glittered in Forester's eyes as he peered at Silverbird. Shania appeared on the verge of rushing to the youth, but her father held out a restraining hand. Harlow edged a step closer to the girl.

Banner uttered a humorless laugh. "Those clothes belong to the real spook, right, Harlow?"

Harlow's eyes narrowed. "You're loco, Banner. Never seen 'em before."

"Found them with your belongin's. Even if I hadn't, I know you're the one behind the killin's."

Harlow shifted his feet and a muscle

twitched near his eye. His gaze darted from Shania to Forester, who was looking at him with a glint of suspicion.

"That's crazy talk, Banner. You got the real killer right there." He jabbed a finger at Silverbird and the 'breed's lips tightened into a hard line. The foreman's voice held a worried edge, now.

"You'd best explain yourself, Banner," said Forester.

"I aim to." Banner took a step closer to Harlow but was still a good six feet from him. He didn't care for the arrangement. Harlow stood too close to Forester and his daughter. That would prove risky if Harlow panicked.

"You see," Banner continued, "I took me a look at the body your 'hand discovered at the arroyo earlier today."

Forester nodded. "Hinkley told me about it, said he didn't know who it was and you'd tend to it."

Banner nodded. "It was Johnny Diller. He hadn't been dead more than two hours."

Forester's eyes widened. "Diller, dead?"

"He disappeared the other night. Way I see it, Harlow and Franklin intended to blame him all along. That's why they let him go around shootin' off his mouth. When I showed up in town and went to search Diller's place it occurred to Harlow he could kill me in the same fashion as the ranchers, then blame Diller, though sooner than they planned. I got away and Franklin had probably already rounded up Diller, so they kept him, figurin' to leave him at Sharpe's and hang him for the killin's. Their luck changed when Silverbird stumbled on to the scene. They took advantage of the fact and framed him. But that made Diller useless to their plan, so Franklin killed him, dumped the body in the arroyo."

"That's some windy, Banner." Harlow edged closer to Shania. Banner caught the move but wasn't in the position to counter it. "But you ain't got a lick of proof."

Banner considered the situation. He needed to keep Harlow talking long enough to get between him and the girl. "I got those clothes. Found them tucked nice and neat in a strongbox in your trunk."

"Anyone might have put it there, maybe even you. I never owned no strongbox."

"I got more than that. Got me a friend who works for the Pinkertons. Sent him a wire and he checked on you and Franklin. One thing surprised me, Harlow. Seems you got a history of avoidin' rustlin' charges. Franklin, now, he had all sorts of things on his record. None of 'em ever stuck, but not a one involved cattle stealin'. Did indicate a few connections to Indian Territory, so I reckon he arranged payoffs. With his connections you could easily dispose of siphoned cattle, even make a handsome profit, though that wasn't enough for you."

Anger washed into Harlow's eyes. "Speculation, Banner, pure and simple."

"Maybe, but you're mighty slick at havin' charges not stick yourself. Two run-ins with rustlin' in New Mex., both of which you got out of because 'evidence' turned up on someone else. That how Franklin turned up charges on Diller?"

Harlow remained silent, but hate came into his eyes.

Banner slid forward a step. "After I saw that I put together the rest of the pieces. You see, by default Forester got all the land and cattle. That makes him top dog in the Panhandle. You planned on killin' him last. How would you do it? Poison? Accident on the range? Happens every day, don't it?" Banner saw the foreman's agitation swell. He took another step, placing himself between Harlow and Silverbird, but not close enough to shield Shania and Forester.

"You're talkin' through your hat," Harlow accused with no conviction. Forester's face registered deep suspicion and Shania was glaring at Harlow.

"Am I? Don't think so. Fact is, anything happens to Forester Shania would inherit the whole bundle. But she's a woman and rightly wouldn't be given much respect runnin' a huge cattle spread in the Panhandle. That's what you'd be counting on. But if you was to be married to her . . ."

Harlow made his move then. It came swiftly, without warning, and even Banner hadn't expected it quite so soon.

He dived sideways and swept an arm around Shania's waist, pinning her to his chest. He drew his gun in nearly the same motion, placing it to her temple. "You're too nosy for anybody's good, Banner. We had it all figured. Everyone would have blamed Diller 'cause his brother got hanged and that would have been that. I would have been somebody, no more rinky-dink rustlin' and sellin' to the Injuns."

What happened next Banner didn't anticipate. He expected a possible move from Silverbird, but he was effectively between him and the killer. The move came from Forester. What possessed him was beyond the manhunter, but he reckoned the rancher's fear for his daughter's life overcame his good sense. He went for Harlow and the foreman swung his gun, triggering a shot. The cattleman jerked, a slug ploughing into his shoulder, throwing him backwards. Harlow spun Shania around, dragged her out into the night.

Banner was powerless to do anything without risking the girl's life.

"Christamighty!" bellowed Forester, gaining his feet. "Don't let him — "

From the corner of his eye, Banner caught movement. Silverbird pulled his gun and was heading for the door. Banner heard hoofbeats and knew Harlow had stolen his horse.

"Silverbird, don't!" he yelled, but the Indian youth was already through the door.

"What's that damn fool doing?" Forester yelled gripping his shoulder, which streamed blood.

245

"Reckon he'll get himself killed to save your daughter, Forester. At least give him the respect he deserves for that."

Forester grunted. "Maybe I was too harsh on him."

"Let's hope you get the chance to tell him that."

Banner dashed for the door, Caleb Forester a beat behind. Harlow had ridden off into the night. He saw Silverbird halfway to the bunkhouse, charging after him.

Banner ran to the livery and saddled a horse in record time. He swung into the saddle while Forester, handicapped by his bad shoulder, fumbled with a mount. The manhunter heeled the horse into a gallop. The moon brightened the grounds and he saw both riders, Harlow ahead by a good 500 yards. Harlow appeared intent on a particular direction — the arroyo, if Banner guessed correctly. He would plan on being followed and would seek refuge in the rocks and brush, keep his pursuers

246

at bay while threatening the girl.

A shot split the night. Harlow had swung around and triggered a shot at Silverbird. The 'breed had closed the distance because Harlow was burdened by Shania.

The slug missed, but next time Silverbird might not be so lucky. The horse Banner had chosen was fast but he was too far behind to prevent anything at this point and Harlow would be too much for an inexperienced youth like Silverbird. He'd damn near killed Banner twice.

The manhunter chanced a backward look, seeing Forester pulling up the rear. He gave the rancher credit for heart, if not sense.

The arroyo. Harlow closed the distance and it appeared he would reach his chosen sanctuary.

Silverbird drew closer and Harlow took another shot at him. Banner cursed, gaining a little yardage himself, but not enough.

Harlow reached the arroyo and

swung from his horse, dragging the young woman, who screeched and kicked, up the arroyo's slope. Silverbird drew up next, leaping from the saddle. Another shot ripped out and Banner saw Silverbird dive for cover.

Banner made the arroyo and was out of his saddle before his horse came to a stop. Crouching, gun drawn, he scurried for cover. He saw movement ahead and squinted, trying to pick out who it was. Harlow. The foreman was on his way to the top of the arroyo, aiming for the protective cover of cottonwoods and brush skirting the fissure's edge. At the pinnacle, the drop to the canyon floor exceeded fifty feet. The manhunter had an idea Harlow had taken the notion to lure Silverbird there, manoeuvre him close to the edge by using Shania as bait, then force him off. That would end one threat and he'd be left with Banner and Forester, who was damn near useless with a bum shoulder.

Banner found himself in a poor

position, one he wasn't used to. He preferred to corner criminals alone, make his own circumstances. Harlow had dealt the cards this time, no doubt knew Banner's operating procedure well. He held all the aces.

A flash of movement to his right broke his reverie.

Silverbird! The 'breed shot from cover and scrambled after Harlow. No choice, Banner moved forward, picking his way up the slope. A chill rode his spine as he glanced at the stream flowing below.

Harlow stopped. Outlined in moonlight he jerked the gun to Shania's temple.

Silverbird halted as well, gun drawn, body rigid.

Banner slowed up about twenty feet behind them, moving cautiously, careful to make no sound. He waited for the foreman's next move. He had little choice.

"You're a fool, Silverbird!" shouted Harlow, a malicious turn on his lips, an insane look in his eyes.

Silverbird muttered something Banner couldn't catch but he heard Harlow laugh and shift his gun towards the youth. In a moment Silverbird would die and Banner could do nothing to stop it.

Harlow's attention on the 'breed, Shania suddenly let out a blood-curdling screech and raked Harlow's shin with her heel. She sank her teeth deep into the foreman's arm and fought to pull free.

Harlow let out a bleat but kept his hold on the girl, whose teeth were still embedded in his arm.

Silverbird lunged. He crashed into both Shania and Harlow, knocking them off balance. The foreman lost his hold on the girl. Shania stumbled away, foot slipping on the lip of the arroyo.

She went down, gripping handfuls of grass, dangling over the edge. A shrill scream tore from her lips. Her hold was tenuous, faltering. In another minute she would plunge to her death.

Silverbird hit Harlow and the foreman's gun flew from his grip. The 'breed lost his own piece and it tumbled over the arroyo's edge, splashing in the stream below.

Shania kept screaming, struggling to pull herself up, losing ground.

Banner, in motion, the moment Silverbird charged Harlow, aimed for her.

Harlow swung a fist that clacked from Silverbird's jaw. The youth staggered back just as Banner reached the scene. The manhunter sidestepped but Harlow dived at him before he could draw aim with his Peacemaker, clearly aware the youth offered little threat compared to the bounty hunter.

The move caught him off-guard. Harlow clouted him full force against the jaw. His Peacemaker spun out of his grip, landing in the grass a few feet away.

Stunned, he nearly went down. His legs turned rubbery and Harlow threw a punch that rattled his senses. He fought a wave of blackness.

By then, Jim Silverbird had gained his feet and rushed to Shania's aide. Too late! Her grip faltered and she went down!

Silverbird dived, slamming into the ground, hand outstretched. He caught her fingertips, snapping her fall short. She hung by a thread and he dug his toes into the soft earth, pushing forward as much as was safe. He locked his other hand around her wrist, but it took every ounce of strength he had to hold on to her. His muscles quivered; in a moment they would fail him. He gritted his teeth, marbles of muscle standing out on either side of his jaw.

"Hold on!" he yelled, straining to pull her up.

"I-I can't! I can't! Help me, Jim! Please help me!" She groped for his hand and caught it, and he pulled harder, letting out a mighty grunt. He almost lost her. Palms slick with sweat, his fingers slipped a notch.

Shania screamed and kicked out, managing to jam a heel into the cliff wall and shove upward.

The extra push was all he needed. He gave it everything he had and jerked her up, hand over hand on her arm until he pulled the top half of her body over the lip. She grabbed his sleeves and clung to him, kicking herself up all the way. The 'breed gained his feet and pulled her into his arms just as Forester gained the top.

Immediate danger passed, their attention shifted to Banner and Harlow. Silverbird pushed Shania towards her father and dropped to his knees, searching for a gun.

Banner fought to keep his senses. His head reeled but with a deep breath his legs steadied.

Harlow rushed him again.

Instinct taking over, the manhunter twisted and brought his leg up, planting a bootheel square in Harlow's bread-basket. The foreman let out an explosive burst of air and staggered.

Banner felt unsteady but determined not to let the foreman get the upper hand again. He lunged, throwing a looping punch that took Harlow square across the jaw. Harlow took a double-step backwards, drawing dangerously close to the edge of the arroyo. He tottered and Banner started for him before he could reorient himself.

A shot sounded, startling, thunderous. Harlow skipped backwards, arms wind-milling. The youth, on his knees had located Banner's Peacemaker and pulled the trigger. The bullet had taken Harlow dead-centre in the chest. The foreman lost his footing and stepped off the edge into thin air. He plunged down in silence.

They heard a splash sound from below.

Banner walked over to Silverbird and took his gun from the boy's loose grip. He gave him a pat on the shoulder and looked at Forester, who bowed his head. Shania ran to Silverbird and they held each other while Banner and Forester slowly walked towards their horses.

* * *

The day was sunny and warm, a perfect day for a wedding. Forester, for all his blustering about Indians, had done it up in style. A band played a slow Mexican tune while guests chattered and sampled from tables holding platters of food. The parlor was festooned with flowers and banners, even a white carpet that flowed to the front door and across the veranda. Sunlight cascaded through the huge windows and sparkled from glasses bubbling with champagne. A huge wedding cake sat in the center of the dining-table, elegant, painstakingly decorated. Servants scurried about, making sure of last-minute preparations.

The main event was scheduled to begin in a few minutes and Banner located Caleb Forester, arm in a sling, standing by the huge double windows.

Normally the manhunter didn't stick around for happy endings, but this one seemed different. He saw a piece of himself in the Indian boy and Shania, a chance he never had. If there was any warmth left inside him, that found it.

Forester glanced at him, turned back to the window. "I still ain't too all-fired happy about this, Banner. I don't like Injuns any better than I did before, but, by damn, that boy's got my respect."

Banner nodded, a thin smile on his lips. "He saved her life. Weren't for him, Harlow might have killed her and got away. He might have killed us all."

Forester turned and looked at the manhunter with resignation in his eyes. He was coming to terms with his hate and Banner reckoned there might be hope for him yet.

"I'll see to it Silverbird gets all I promised Harlow. He'll have his spread plus enough to set him and Shania for life. Found out Sharpe had some relatives back East, two, a cousin and half-brother. I wired them and they'll be comin' out here to take over Sharpe's spread. Reckon I have too much and I suddenly got no desire to see my name up with the likes of Chisum and the rest. Got all I need long as Shania's happy and alive."

Forester had humbled, that was evident, and Banner liked him a whole lot better, now.

"You're doin' the right thing, Forester. Ain't easy to admit when you're wrong."

Forester cast him a serious look. "Reckon it's a whole lot easier than to lose the person you love most."

Banner nodded, a longing tugging at his heart. "What about Bob Diller?"

Forester peered at the floor, back to Banner. "Reckon that's somethin' I'll spend a lifetime atoning for. Boys didn't have any other family. What else can I do?"

"Some mistakes can't be fixed. Just see to it you give Silverbird and your daughter your best."

Forester nodded, slapping the man-hunter's shoulder. "What about you, Banner?"

He shrugged. "Already got me another job up Colorada way. Aim to head out right after the weddin'."

"You won't stick around? I could offer you a parcel of land, a few thousand head to get you started."

Banner laughed with perverse humor. "There was time I would have gladly accepted that offer. Now it's too late. Reckon that's somethin' I'll never atone for."

He walked off, leaving Caleb Forester staring after him.

THE END

FIGHTING RAMROD
Charles N. Heckelmann

Most men would have cut their losses, but Frazer counted the bullets in his guns and said he'd soak the range in blood before he'd give up another inch of what was his.

LONE GUN
Eric Allen

Smoke Blackbird had been away too long. The Lequires had seized the Blackbird farm, forcing the Indians and settlers off, and no one seemed willing to fight! He had to fight alone.

THE THIRD RIDER
Barry Cord

Mel Rawlins wasn't going to let anything stand in his way. His father was murdered, his two brothers gone. Now Mel rode for vengeance.

ARIZONA DRIFTERS
W. C. Tuttle

When drifting Dutton and Lonnie Steelman decide to become partners they find that they have a common enemy in the formidable Thurston brothers.

TOMBSTONE
Matt Braun

Wells Fargo paid Luke Starbuck to outgun the silver-thieving stagecoach gang at Tombstone. Before long Luke can see the only thing bearing fruit in this eldorado will be the gallows tree.

HIGH BORDER RIDERS
Lee Floren

Buckshot McKee and Tortilla Joe cut the trail of a border tough who was running Mexican beef into Texas. They stopped the smuggler in his tracks.

BRETT RANDALL, GAMBLER
E. B. Mann

Larry Day had the choice of running away from the law or of assuming a dead man's place. No matter what he decided he was bound to end up dead.

THE GUNSHARP
William R. Cox

The Eggerleys weren't very smart. They trained their sights on Will Carney and Arizona's biggest blood bath began.

THE DEPUTY OF SAN RIANO
Lawrence A. Keating and
Al. P. Nelson

When a man fell dead from his horse, Ed Grant was spotted riding away from the scene. The deputy sheriff rode out after him and came up against everything from gunfire to dynamite.

FARGO: MASSACRE RIVER
John Benteen

The ambushers up ahead had now blocked the road. Fargo's convoy was a jumble, a perfect target for the insurgents' weapons!

SUNDANCE: DEATH IN THE LAVA
John Benteen

The Modoc's captured the wagon train and its cargo of gold. But now the halfbreed they called Sundance was going after it . . .

HARSH RECKONING
Phil Ketchum

Five years of keeping himself alive in a brutal prison had made Brand tough and careless about who he gunned down . . .

FARGO: PANAMA GOLD
John Benteen

With foreign money behind him, Buckner was going to destroy the Panama Canal before it could be completed. Fargo's job was to stop Buckner.

FARGO:
THE SHARPSHOOTERS
John Benteen

The Canfield clan, thirty strong were raising hell in Texas. Fargo was tough enough to hold his own against the whole clan.

PISTOL LAW
Paul Evan Lehman

Lance Jones came back to Mustang for just one thing — revenge! Revenge on the people who had him thrown in jail.